ABOUT THE AUTHOR

Jennifer Manson is a writer and business woman. She lives in Christchurch, New Zealand, with her husband, two teenage children and two cats. She is the author of *The Moment of Change*, *Tasha Stuart interviews . . .*, *The Old Occidental Writers' Hotel* and *Law of Attraction* and also writes for *The Press* newspaper's "at home" supplement.

Slow Time

Jennifer Manson

ACKNOWLEDGEMENTS

To my writing buddy, poet Kerrin P. Sharpe;

To my proof reader Vicki Slade and my editor Tanya Tremewan;

To John Law, ex-Mayor of Rodney District, who was responsible for Matakana becoming New Zealand's first official Slow Town – for your commitment to making the world a better place for people to live in;

To Bill Strickland, founder of the Manchester Bidwell Center in Pittsburgh and author of *Make the Impossible Possible*, for your uplifting vision;

To Lynley Maxwell, my beautiful account manager at PrintStop+, Manchester St, Christchurch, for your amazing service;

To the people at the heart of The Café de Paris in Hokitika, for making it worth a journey from Wanaka, Christchurch, wherever;

To Janet and Martyn Thomas, for your support, encouragement and excellent hospitality – the château is on its way;

To Diane Gardiner, for many hours of wonderful conversation, and for introducing me to your West Highland Terrier, Archie;

To Carl Honoré, for bringing the concept of Slow to the wide world;

To my daughter, Alex, my son, Jono, and my wonderful husband, Paul;

Thank you.

1

I am tired. So tired.

I thought that after my exams, my final assignments were over, I would go back to my flat, settle in for another summer of working the city cafés, enjoy the sun and my friends and the life of Christchurch, my adopted home town. But I just want to go home. I want to sleep and never wake up, never have to do anything, ever again.

I let a lot of people down, but waitresses are ten a penny, they'd find another one in no time.

"There's nobody like you, Jo," they argued.

"Yeah, right."

What was I doing working in a café anyway? I'd overheard myself described as the star of my year, business administration and economics. I could have been starting a long career with one of the big accounting firms, or maybe in an oil company's management trainee programme.

"Are you thinking of post-graduate study? Come and see me if you are, I'd be happy to supervise you." Coming from more than one lecturer, it was a big compliment. But I thought I'd go mad if I tried to think about the future, this soon after surviving the relentless pressure of the recent past.

I caught the bus to Folkstown carrying only my backpack. My best friend was passing through on her way home to Wanaka in just a few days, she'd bring the heavy stuff.

Folkstown is a pretty little place, nothing special, but a great stopping-off point for anyone going from somewhere to somewhere else. A vision of the main street, full of smiling faces, eased into my mind. I put the little bag between my head and the window and fell instantly asleep.

"Anybody home?"

The house was as chaotic as always – more so: it seemed Dad had taken to repairing his chainsaws right in the middle of the living room, there was oil everywhere, chain links on the sofa, screws and, oddly, a chisel scattered on the glass coffee table, a recent copy of GQ staring incongruously up through it from the lower shelf. An open toolbox on the floor could have been a deliberate burglar deterrent. If there were any burglars in Folkstown.

"Dad? Grandad? Anyone?"

I hadn't really expected them to be in, but I was disappointed anyway. Some kind of homecoming. I went through to my bedroom, the only organised space in the house, and turned on the electric blanket despite the warm spring day. I had been cold, tired and hungry for a month; if I wasn't going to get fed right away – and a glance into the kitchen made me automatically recoil – at least I could get warm, sleep a little.

I picked up my toothbrush but the bathroom was too daunting to tackle just yet. They'd get on it once they knew I was here. They're a couple of old bachelors, my paternal forebears, but they like to think they know how to treat a lady.

I took out a wet wipe and slid off my make-up, barely giving my face time to dry before it hit the pillow. Sleep came rapidly once more.

SLOW TIME

2

When there's nothing to do, do nothing.

Dad stared at me across a forkful of the stew he'd magically produced from the slow-cooker. His concern was gradually congealing into anger as I failed to answer his questions to his satisfaction.

"It must be more than that. You look dreadful. Is it drugs?"

"No, Dad, I've just been working hard. Studying. I'm going to do really well in my exams. First Class Honours, without a doubt."

He grunted and glanced at Grandad. "Dark circles, thin and pale as a ghost." He seemed to be talking to himself more than me. "Probably even lost your sense of humour."

"Why don't you try me, Dad? Tell me a joke."

Grandad chuckled briefly but was silenced by a look from his son-in-law. "I'm not kidding. There's something wrong with you, something serious. Is this why you didn't come home last holidays? Are you sick?"

"Dad, I had a job. I told you. I'm fine. Just been busy. You know me, when there's anything more interesting going on, I forget to eat. That's all it is. And I haven't been sleeping so well."

He grunted again in triumph. "I knew it! Drugs! One to come up, another to come down."

"Dad, shut up. You really don't know what you're talking about. I haven't been sleeping, but now I'm home, I'll be fine." These, I knew, were the magic words. The pair of them started clucking around like a couple of hens, filling my water glass, pushing more bread onto my plate. "This stew is really great, Dad. When did you get the slow-cooker?"

He took up the new subject, selected at random as a distraction, with an unexpected passion. "Slow Food!" he said. "It's a revolution."

Grandad and I did the dishes. Dad was supposed to be clearing away the bits of chainsaw, but from the sound of it he'd got distracted tinkering again. Ten minutes later it started up, deafening through the thin walls. "Dad! Not in the house!" It stopped, and there was a sheepish silence then the sound of the toolbox clicking shut. A minute later I heard the outside door open and close.

I turned and grinned at Grandad. "Well, at least that hasn't changed. Who'd have thought it, though, Dad cooking? I thought I'd never wean him off nightly junk food. Josie's will probably close without him."

Something flickered across the old man's face. "Josie's is closed already."

"No! Why? Did she get sick or something? Win the lottery?" Grandad's face told me not to be flip, but I couldn't help it. Josie's was so much part of the town it felt like the earth had shifted under my feet.

"The town's not doing so great, Jo. Lots of people aren't doing so well."

"Why, what do you mean? What happened?"

"Maybe your dad should explain it. You know I don't always get things right."

I took the tea towel out of his hands and led him back to the kitchen table.

"You tell me, please?"

"Well, they say it's that navigation."

"Navigation?"

"That they have in cars now."

I didn't really understand, but I didn't want to hurt his feelings. "What about it?"

"More of the cars have it now, you see. Almost all the rental cars. And it tells them to go around the town, go a different way. The tourists aren't coming here any more. Not so many of them, anyway."

I was beginning to understand. Folkstown was a stop-off between the major tourist sights. Or it had been. It wasn't on the shortest route, but it was close, and hundreds of tourists passed through each day, stopping for lunch or coffee or petrol or souvenirs. Could something this simple make a difference? I felt an eerie chill pass through me. Yes, it could.

"Tell me what's happening, Grandad."

"Lots of things. They've cut down my hours at the petrol station, said they can't afford to pay me so much."

I looked into his face, at the tears in the corners of his eyes. He'd been working there since he was fourteen. How could his minimum wage make a difference? "I don't get it. I don't understand."

"They're selling less petrol. Giles said 10% less, or 12."

7

I knew the figures wouldn't mean much to him, but I did some quick calculations. Tourists probably made up around 50% of the fuel sales, so that meant 20 or 25% fewer tourists passing through. Some of the shops were 90% tourist trade - the souvenir shops, the lunch places. And the owners of those shops spent money in the rest of the town. 20% fewer tourists represented much of the profit, and probably all of the luxuries for the whole town. This was a catastrophe.

"What's being done?"

He looked at me blankly. I felt a moment of unfair impatience, forced myself to give him a brief smile before pushing past him to the door.

"Dad! Dad! Come in here."

3

My dad and grandad both lost their wives the same year. Grandma went first, when I was seven. That was hard, but it made sense, kind of. Grandad moved in with us, and three months later Mum was killed by a motorist speeding through town. She and I were on the pedestrian crossing coming home from school. She pushed me out of the way and didn't make it herself. That was harder. It's a small town and everyone was in mourning, with me at the centre. Every mother was at my side, with there-but-for-the-grace-of-God guilt and gratitude; I became the town's adopted daughter, which I kind of liked, and kind of couldn't stand.

Dad disappeared in the intensity of it, succumbing to his private grief, relieved that I was the focus, staying in the shadows. The only thing I really saw of it was in the kindness he showed Grandad. Grandad always needed looking after, and there was no-one now to do it but him.

Now his resignation infuriated me. Question after question elicited barely more than shrugs.

"What can we do, Jo? There's nothing we can do. Just tighten our belts and wait to come through this. Things have been hard before."

"Dad, this isn't going away. This isn't like a strong dollar or a terrorist attack in some other part of the world, so that the tourists stop coming for a while, but later come back. This will be permanent."

I watched my words sink in. His face had been tired, drawn, sad. Now his eyes set into a dead nothing. I wanted to shake him. "Come on, Dad. Wake up."

He stood up slowly, shoulders rising to the level of his ears. I hadn't seen him truly angry since the night I came home at four a.m. after the year eleven disco on the back of Bryan Smith's motorbike. I bit my lip, waiting for him to speak, to yell, something.

"You're the financial genius," he whispered, with terrifying restraint. "You fix it."

I rolled over, burying my face in my pillow. I just wanted rest, sweet rest, and now I couldn't turn off my thoughts. After a night of fruitless searching for answers I dragged myself out of bed to begin my usual homecoming rounds, visiting all my surrogate mothers. The sun was shining but I felt bleak as I tacked on the necessary smile.

Josie's was boarded up. I should have asked Dad where she had gone, what she was doing now, but as I hadn't I decided to try her house.

It had the same neglected air as the shop, grass grown long, a broken window at the front taped together, barely holding. I knocked on the screen door, which rattled against the frame. No answer. It squeaked as I pulled it back to try the door, unlocked. "Josie?" Inside it was dark, uncared for, but not cold enough to be empty. "Hey, anyone home?"

A voice creaked from a back bedroom. "Joanna? Is that you?"

"Yeah. Hey."

"Just give me a minute, I'll be out."

I waited, looking round, resisting the urge to start tidying. Well, maybe I could just stack up that newspaper. I was still smoothing out the pages and putting them in order when Josie appeared in the doorway, blinking. "My God, what time is it? When did you get back?"

I would have hugged her, but that's not the sort of woman she is; and probably I'd have wanted to wait till she had a shower anyway.

"Yesterday. How are you?"

Her eyebrows flicked upwards. "Oh, you know. On the dole, lost everything. You?"

On the bus yesterday I'd had a little fantasy, of sitting at this dining table, crying out my woes of overwork and too many choices. What a brat!

"Why don't you go have a shower? I'll make you breakfast."

"No hot water. Boiler's broken."

"Well, have a cold one. You'll feel better. I'll boil some water in the kettle so you can wash your hair."

Grumbling, but with the beginnings of a smile, she shuffled back through to the hallway. Shame it took a dead mother to give me this much influence.

I ran my fingers through my hair, wondering where to start. I turned on the lights in the living room and the kitchen and pulled the curtains wide open. Sunlight was striking the budding trees on the road opposite, a note of hope. I filled the kettle and surveyed my surroundings. She must hate living like this. Despite the grease in the air of her takeaway shop, everything was always clean, wiped down at the end of every day, and compulsively several times a day in between, whenever there was a lull in orders and her hands weren't busy. Her hands were always busy.

I carried through the kettle. She was arranging a mismatched pile of clean clothes on the chair next to the overflowing hamper.

I poured it into the hand basin and mixed in some cold.

"Don't worry about that, there's no shampoo."

"I'll bring the dishwashing detergent. It'll do just this once."

"Jo . . ."

"Don't argue, I don't think either of us have the energy for it."

She stared at me a moment, then subsided. I brought the liquid and a second jug of hot water and left her to it. Back in the kitchen I opened the window and back door and felt a cleansing breeze begin to flow. I loaded the ancient dishwasher, took the rubbish bag out to the bin outside. It felt good to be doing something practical, something away from my books. The wider questions of last night still hummed in the background, but I felt more hopeful now.

"That really does feel better. And look what you've done out here." She smiled for a moment, then her eyes misted over. What happened to the strong people I left behind a year ago?

"It's okay, Josie. It really is."

"No, Honey, it isn't. But it's nice of you to say."

"Don't give up! You can't give up."

A tiny shrug. "I sort of already have."

I hesitated, close to defeat myself. I reached over and picked up my bag from where I'd hung it over a chair. "Come on. We're going out. Coffee. My treat."

I waited outside while Josie pulled the door behind us. I noticed she didn't lock up. "Where do you want to go?"

I had meant it to be a joke – we always went to Louise's – but for a moment she hesitated. I didn't ask why. I guessed I'd find out when we got there. We fell into step, forgetting to talk as we both lost ourselves in our thoughts.

SLOW TIME

4

Louise had been my mum's best friend when they were at school. Both her children were boys so she had been eager to step up when I needed advice on girl stuff: make-up and periods and clothes, enjoying the opportunity to do the things her own children didn't need.

I had worked in her café when it was still a tearoom, helping her with the adaptation to the new times when it became clear a café was the way to the future.

Before I even got in the door I could feel the difference. There was a row of flies along the front ledge, and the way the light inside her smiley-face sign flickered, like it was in its death throes, made me want to cry. Josie looked at me and pulled her chin in close before opening the door. We walked in and I wanted to walk right out again. My chest constricted and I had to force my eyes to stay open.

There was no-one in sight. The lights were dim. A postcard stand encroached near my shoulder, its contents curled and damp. The once-bright food cabinets were empty, a few dog-eared menus lying on top.

"How is she still open? Why?"

"Louise?" Josie yelled. "You have customers."

There was no answer. I looked around for something I could do, some way to make even a minor difference, but there was nothing. The tears did come now. "How could things have got so bad so fast?"

"She was suffering already, after they opened that new barn of a place down the road the year before last. But she kept going for the locals." Josie shrugged. "Just like me, the downward slide is pretty fast once it starts. At least . . ." She stopped speaking as we heard a noise out back. "Louise?"

She came bustling through with a startled expression. "I'm sorry, I was ..." She stopped as she realised who it was. Her eyes rested on me, scared, scattered, "No, oh no!" then came into focus as she looked accusingly at Josie. "How could you bring her in here? No warning, nothing!" She turned around and disappeared out back again. Josie and I looked at each other for a moment then followed.

"Louise, Honey, it's okay. We're here to help."

She was slumped over the Formica table in the corner where I used to sit with my colouring books when Mum was alive. I had helped out at the counter so she and Louise could gossip. I had learned so much about life at that table, about relationships, about men, even though it was years before I could put it all in context.

I put my hand on her hair, feeling her anguish sob up through my arm. She kept her face hidden, and after a minute or two the tears slowed. There was even half a smile as she finally turned towards me. "I was holding it together before you showed up."

"Why? Why were you? What was the point?"

Again that confused expression, a vague, indecisive movement. "Because . . ." she shook her head and her shoulders slumped again. She looked like a wild animal, captured and put in a zoo. She had given all the fight she had and now she was exhausted. My bottom lip pulled downwards, but I wasn't going to let her see me cry.

"Come on. You're closing."

"What do you mean?"

"I mean, you're closing. What's the point in staying open when no-one comes here? You must be losing money every day."

Louise just stared at me. Josie hovered nervously. After thirty seconds of impasse I turned and looked around me. There was a stack of newsprint on the counter. I hunted till I found a black marker pen, some masking tape. I have compulsively neat writing, a throwback to a great great grandfather who was a ship's record-keeper and historical artist. I wrote in large letters. "Closed until further notice. Sorry for any inconvenience."

I stuck it in the window. "There, that's done. Now, we need to get you some way to live. Where are the boys? What are they doing?" Louise was still staring blankly. Josie answered.

"Bill's away in Christchurch with his dad. He's working in a supermarket. Jason'll be finishing up his exams soon. He comes in after school to help out."

Poor kid! "We'll get you a Work and Income appointment. You'll need a benefit till you work things out." I picked up the phone: disconnected. How had she even taken payment? No phone line meant no card payments, and who carried cash nowadays?

There were so many questions, but she wasn't in a state to answer them. I hesitated over what to do next: talk or do. Either was probably going to be beyond her, but at least if Josie and I were doing something, she could join in when she felt like it. I handed Josie a cloth. "Start wiping tables. I'll be back soon."

It took twenty minutes to navigate the 0800 system and plead my way to an appointment for the next day that the local Work and Income office was open: once a week, on Mondays, short hours. I had to use my best assertive voice and bandy around terms like "at risk" which I knew they had to respond to. It felt like betrayal; Louise would hate it. But it had to be done. I skipped into the supermarket on the way back, picked up a loaf of bread, cheese, chocolate.

"Here, I'll make a cuppa. Cut us some sandwiches?"

After a little hunting I found three clean cups, tea bags. There were five large bottles of milk; she must still be getting her standard order. I'd have to remember to cancel it. The Zip was hot and in five minutes we were sitting at a freshly wiped table feeling better with some food inside us. I hadn't eaten since last night.

"How's that boy of yours doing? Still the sports star?"

Louise's eyes lifted with instinctive enthusiasm. "He played on the provincial team this winter. They want him to try out for the Crusaders, can you believe it?"

"Sure I can. He's amazing."

"Course, that'd mean he'd leave, too."

"Well, it's not so far away."

"Yeah." Her dull eyes fell on the table again. "And he'd be better off."

I swallowed. Words failed. I pushed my chair back from the table. "Come on. Work to do. Let's get this place looking spotless."

Both women turned to me now, as if they feared I might be losing it. Not yet, I thought, but I have to keep going, keep doing something, or I just might.

Where should we start? I took a deep breath and held it. Anywhere, just start anywhere. Do the first obvious thing, then the next, then the next. The next step is always clear once you get there. I had to believe that.

"Let's stack up the tables, make some space. Then we can mop the floor." Josie and Louise were still staring at me, blank, motionless. I picked up the table nearest the corner and placed it against the wall. Josie helped me with the next one, we tipped it upside down and stacked it on top of the first. "Louise, can you get some hot water in a bucket?" Long seconds passed, then finally she began to move, slowly, into an upright position, her steps sluggishly accelerating as she headed for the back room. Josie turned back to me and opened her mouth to speak.

"Say nothing. Just keep going." It was all I could do to keep from falling apart myself.

SLOW TIME

5

I brought Louise back to eat with us at home. After one beat of surprise Dad greeted her as if it were an everyday occurrence. His eyes strayed for a second to her untidy hair, her un-ironed clothes but he said nothing, just motioned to a chair, brought her a cup of tea.

"Dad's got a slow-cooker. He's a master chef now."

Louise raised her eyes in automatic acknowledgement. I wasn't sure if she'd heard me.

"Jason will be by later, I left him a note. We got enough, Dad?"

"Sure. The more the merrier." His voice was bright with overdone cheer. He stood staring for a few seconds, then excused himself to put some washing in the machine. I looked around. He'd made good progress with the house while I'd been gone, it was almost presentable.

"No work today?" I asked as he came back into the room.

"No. Got some pruning tomorrow, then some power-line clearance later in the week. I hate that indiscriminate hacking, but it's got to be done I suppose."

"You'd rather it was trees before technology, I know, Dad."

"Well, the trees were there first." It was his old argument with the world, and he spoke out of habit.

"I know, Dad, you don't have to convert me."

Grandad came in then, and the conversation got easier. He was pleased to see Louise, and showed no surprise. She thawed a little at his warm greeting and roused herself to answer his questions, until they turned to the café.

"We closed the café today, Grandad," I interjected.

"Why did you do that?"

Dad also turned to me in surprise, waiting for my answer.

"It wasn't doing so well. It's just to give Louise time to decide what to do. You own the building, that's right isn't it, Louise? No mortgage?"

She took a moment to let the question sink in, then nodded.

"So she has lots of options. She needs a bit of a break, then she can decide."

Grandad nodded, but Dad turned away, a look of deep sadness on his face. I wanted to tell him it would be all right, but the words wouldn't come. There had to be some way out of this, but I couldn't see it yet.

"Well." Grandad patted her hand. "It's good you're having a bit of a holiday. You deserve one after all that hard work."

She looked like she might be going to cry, then laughed instead. She put a hand up to his face. "You're a good man." She nodded. "Such a good man."

There was a beep from the kitchen. "Dinner's ready. Everybody wash up now."

Jason joined us half way through the meal, taking a plate and squeezing in between Grandad and me. I guessed he had delayed going home after his exam. He couldn't have been expecting much of a reception. His smile was slower to come than I remembered, but finally it broke through and his eating accelerated. "This is really good Mr Connors."

Dad grinned. "Thanks. I'll show you how to do it. It's so simple. You nearly finished your exams?"

"Last one today."

"Plans for the summer?"

He threw a quick glance at his mother. "Not sure yet."

We left the older generations clearing up and headed into the main street for a breath of young company. "How are you doing?"

"Oh, you know."

"We closed the café today."

"Yeah, I saw the sign."

"You cool with that?"

"Yeah, I guess. Something needed to happen, but she wouldn't listen to me."

"It will all work out."

He stopped and turned to me. "Will it? Really?" He shook his head.

"There's always a way to pick things up. I have to believe that. My whole degree is based on that fact." I tried a laugh, but it was unconvincing.

His eyebrows arched momentarily and his lips twitched in a pout.

"There are a million things she could do."

"Name three."

"I don't know. Start an internet business. Sell real estate. Do something so amazing that it will actually draw people to the town."

I had seen a hopeful flicker on his face as I started speaking, but he turned away again in disappointment. "I thought you actually had some ideas."

At this, my frustration turned to anger. "I'm back barely twenty-four hours. I wasn't expecting this. Cut me some slack, would you?"

He turned back, eyes remorseful. "I'm sorry, Jo, I'm sorry." It was like he was nine years old again. "It's just so depressing. Half of me just wants to get out, run away, and then I feel guilty for thinking about leaving her the way she is."

"You have to live your life."

His pleading eyes fixed on my face. "It's not that simple. Is it?"

"You have to trust her to be able to work this out."

"Did you really look at her? She's not managing on her own."

"She's tough. She will."

He snorted and rolled his eyes. I stood my ground. He's always been like a little brother to me, and I was used to his theatrics of old. The silence lengthened and I felt hope rising in me. I did believe what I said. There was a way through this. I just had to find it.

"Tell me about the rest of the town. What's happening?"

He tilted his head to the side and back. "Pretty much the same. Not quite as bad as Mum yet, but things are fading all over. The businesses that don't rely directly on tourists are feeling it slower, but it's hitting there, too. Quite a few families have moved away, kids disappearing from school. It's pretty quiet. No going away parties. Sometimes it takes a while to realise someone has gone."

For some reason this was the bleakest news of all. "Old families? People I know?"

"Mostly not, mostly the newer ones. But the Blacks have gone, and the Andersons."

"Oh, God."

"Yeah. But hey, work a miracle and they might come back!"

He was teasing, he must be feeling better; he meant it as a joke but in his words I heard a tiny seed of hope, for all of us.

I woke the next morning and rolled over to revel in the sunlight streaming onto my face. This town is beautiful when the sun shines, at this time of year with the fresh new leaves on the trees, and especially in autumn when the colours are a glorious display, and the snow-covered peaks form a vivid backdrop. I decided to spend the day in bed, doing what I came here to do: rest. I pulled the curtains back further with my toe, then found myself jumping up to remove them altogether. Who cared if old man Sullivan from next door peeked in? I had Grandma's old folding screen I could change behind. For now I wanted all the light going.

I folded the curtains and put them on the floor of the wardrobe. When I had some extra money I'd get them cleaned to put back for the winter; they could stay as they were for now. I climbed back into bed and watched the dust float in golden spirals. I let my thoughts tumble over and over with them, images of the last few weeks, exam rooms blending one into another; dawn through my bedroom window after working all night on an essay; then the more recent scenes: Grandad's face as he talked about the changes in the town; the chaos of Josie's living room; then finally, most haunting of all, Louise's horribly altered face. It was too much. I couldn't make sense of anything with this picture in my mind. I tried to shake it off but it kept returning, the spirals getting smaller and smaller, coming back faster and faster until I couldn't think of anything else.

I threw back the covers once more and went in search of some distraction.

Dad and Grandad were at work. I thought about breakfast, but I wasn't hungry. I emptied the dishwasher, put a load of towels in the washing machine, then sat on a bar stool with my chin on my hand, staring out the window. My thoughts were a little calmer here. The light on Dad's slow-cooker flicked on and I wandered over to peer inside. The cookbook - from the library - was open at a recipe for meatballs. I guessed that's what we were having for dinner that night. Long term all this meat wasn't going to agree with me, but it felt good to eat with the boys for a while, it helped me know I was really home.

I picked up the book to leaf through it. Maybe I could get good at this myself. I flicked it closed, holding my finger in place, to see the cover and title: *The Slow Cooker Cookbook* and as I did so I noticed another library book underneath it: *In Praise of Slow*. I put the recipe book back down, forgetting to hold the page. The second was more interesting. I wandered back to my bedroom and curled up under the covers, already absorbed. Even the introduction grabbed me. "Of course!" I found myself thinking. "This is what I was looking for." Dad had talked about the food, the taste of the food, but this, this complete philosophy, he hadn't mentioned at all.

I devoured the book, reading fast, flicking ahead, paradoxically agreeing but frustrated. It all made sense, but it didn't go nearly far enough. Where was the why? It was one thing to argue against the modern stressed and pressured lifestyle, but there had to be more to the motivation than avoiding something bad. Where was the real payoff? What was the Holy Grail? I suspected it was something you could only know if you really tried it, made a real experiment, not this expedient compromise, with no fundamental change of goals.

At the same time, in the back of my mind, an irony was coming into focus. Folkstown was fading for just the opposite reason: the drive for efficiency, an invisible assumption. Navigation systems were great for making things easier, taking out the stress, removing the front seat arguments that have hounded the travelling public since the first time a map was handed into the passenger seat, often the only situation where otherwise compatible couples would hurl indiscriminate abuse at each other, ending in tears.

I applauded technology that brought peace into relationships once more; but at the same time, something else was lost. Where was the scenic option? Where was the space for choosing the Slow Route? You punch in your destination, the system reads your current location and unless you give it more detailed instruction, it tells you the shortest way there. The fastest.

What if that wasn't what you wanted? You would probably never realise, because the question was never asked. Gravel roads or not gravel roads? But no option for beautiful places to stop along the way. This might change in the future, but in the meantime, it meant the death of our town.

I read on, twisting and turning these ideas in my mind. I could feel something brewing, something that desired action but as yet no action was clear. I threw back the covers again, jumped in the shower, dressed and headed out the door. I needed more information, and I wouldn't find it in my bedroom, or in my quiet view of the sky.

I walked fast, through long-familiar streets to the town. Here were the shops: the petrol station, Grandad too deep in serving petrol to see my cheerful wave; the barn café; the interior design shop; the specialty chocolate shop; the dairy; Josie's boarded-up takeaway; Louise's closed-down café. The pub. The tourist information office. The library. The gift shop. I paced up and down, up and down, somehow taking in every shop front again and again while at the same time watching the tips of my shoes in their rhythmic flashing, left, right, left, right.

A few times a face came into focus, an expression of delight at seeing me. A few times I stopped and answered questions about my family, my progress at university, my non-existent plans. I loved these people, and I pulled myself out of my thoughts as well as I could, took an interest in their lives also. But once they had gone my reverie continued: left, right, left, right. Aha!

6

We'd make Folkstown a Slow Town! This was the answer, I was sure. Remove the excess, remove the hurry, get back to the things that really matter: people, relationships, experiencing the beauty of life. The tourists we were losing only stayed a little while anyway: twenty minutes, half an hour, an hour; grabbed a coffee to wake them up for the drive onwards, or lunch if it happened to be that time of day. Maybe bought a souvenir or two, a locally made (or more often, not locally made) jumper. Then on. Have to get to Queenstown, or Wanaka, or back to Christchurch by tonight.

This Slow movement was a worldwide thing, tapping into fundamental and almost forgotten human desires. If we became a Slow Town, the tourists we'd attract would stay longer: a day, two days, a week. Form real relationships; experience the pace of life and the beauty of the surroundings; remember us and tell their friends, their colleagues, other Slow Time enthusiasts. It could be indescribably easy.

I closed my eyes and saw it all before me; the tree-lined streets, pedestrian friendly; the Slow Food restaurants; a Slow Time hotel; bed and breakfasts; Slow Time workshops; a knitting circle, with local people getting together in the evening to sit and talk and be. No clocks, no television, no rush.

The phrase I had had in my head on the night of my arrival floated back to me:

When there's nothing to do, do nothing.

I didn't even know where it came from, where I'd heard it . . .

That would be our motto.

But how was I going to persuade the whole town to adopt it, put it on their tourist brochures, make it the focus of their international self-promotion?

I closed my eyes again. One thing at a time. First I would go home, finish reading the book, do some internet research. I tried to shut out the other idea that was brewing. This wasn't for me, it was for the people, the town I loved. And I hadn't planned to even think about this for a long while to come. Still, the idea persisted: here, if anywhere, was the subject of my Ph.D.

When there's nothing to do, do nothing. It was such a freeing thought. I looked around Dad's house as I walked in the door and could just let everything be. He was getting to it in his own time. There was plenty of time. I picked up the Slow book and lay on the sofa, where the sun had moved around to rest during this part of the day. It was quiet. My eyes drifted closed and I heard the chime of a bellbird, the hum of a bee, the rise and Doppler fall of the engine of a slowly passing car.

My thoughts drifted, rising above the everyday, connecting the dots of a new existence. I felt the beat of my heart and, as I observed it, I noticed it slow, just a little, barely perceptible. I played with it, beating in time with the nodding of my head, then slowing down, slowing down, felt it slowly follow. It felt good; powerful. I could control the beating of my heart. I let my breath deepen, consciously drawing it deep into my body. I never had patience for yoga, but I remembered someone saying once that you could breathe into any part of the body. It didn't make sense at the time – breath was in the lungs, surely? But now I played with breathing into my gut, my legs, my feet, becoming aware of each part of myself in turn. It was hypnotic. I lost track of time passing, floating in my surroundings, until the sound of the doorknob turning pulled me back.

"Anyone home?"

"Hey, Jason. I'm through here."

"Sleeping in the middle of the afternoon? Lazy!"

His words annoyed me unreasonably, disproportionately. "I'm not being lazy, I'm creating, coming up with a new idea." My mood was broken and I sat up, scowling.

He held up his hands in mock surrender and laughed. "Touchy."

"Shut up. Am I the only one looking for a way out here?"

"Way out of what?" He looked honestly perplexed. It was my turn to laugh.

"Boys! Such short memories! Imminent financial and social ruin. Ring any bells?"

He frowned. "Oh. That. I thought you meant something we could actually do something about."

"Pessimist. Of course we can do something. What's your mum up to today?"

"Nothing. That's sort of why I came out. It's . . ."

"Depressing?"

"Yeah."

"Look, let's go get her. We can talk about what you can do, what she can do in the short term. We just need a holding pattern until we get through this, see the way to something new."

"Is it really that simple?"

"I know things look bad at the moment. Louise isn't herself. But she will be again. She just needs time to adapt."

"Adapt to what?"

"To change."

"But change to what?" His voice rose, desperate and exasperated.

"That's just what I'm trying to say! I don't know yet. Who knows where we'll end up? But I'm working on it. And so can you. And so can she."

He shrugged again, his momentary energy waning, draining out of him. The slump of his shoulders annoyed me. Was I going to have to do this entirely on my own?

7

After an hour with Jason and Louise I'd had enough. It was like they wanted to stay stuck. I knew I couldn't do it for them, I couldn't lift them out of their funk by sheer force of my own will. But that didn't stop me trying. I came home, exasperated with them and with myself. All logic told me they'd come out of it in their own time. I had to be patient. Yeah, right! Great track record I've got in that area.

I banged in through the door, swearing under my breath, and stopped short. Something was different. Grandad was home.

"Hey there. Off work early?"

"Yeah. It took a bit of getting used to, but it's sort of nice working less. I can take more time over things."

That made me laugh. Grandad always took the time he needed over everything. Generations of family members had tried to hurry him, each one finally learning it was much better to go with his flow.

Maybe that's why I liked sitting with Grandad so much – it was relaxing. He didn't always have to be talking, and he had a way of cutting straight to the heart of an issue whatever irrelevancies others had dressed it up with.

He looked up from the chess set he was arranging on the coffee table. "Things aren't so good."

"No."

"But you'll make it all right again, Jo, you're clever, you'll know what to do."

"Thanks, Grandad. Yeah, I think I do know what to do. Now just got to convince everyone else."

"They'll listen to you."

"I hope so."

He went back to the chess pieces, moving them around in the slow dance I'd never been able to figure out the pattern of. When I was ten I used to ask him to play against me, and he'd always refuse with a faint air of failure. "I don't want to play against you, Jo. We're friends, aren't we?"

"It's just a game, Grandad."

He'd shake his head, gently, and sometimes, if I'd really push him, he'd get upset, and the words would burst out of him. "I don't want to fight! I just want things to go along."

The echoing words confused me now as they had confused me then. His lack of logic worried me, and I shook my head, thinking to get rid of it. Then something made me pause. Something in his words chimed with something new in my thoughts. What if he'd been right all along, and the energy I put into competition, into pushing against something to win, could be better channelled?

I went and sat beside him, watching the way the pieces moved in his hands. "What are you doing there, Grandad?"

He looked up, startled. He was usually happiest under the radar. Direct scrutiny made him nervous. I should have known better. "Nothing, Jo. I'm not doing anything at all." He put his hands in his pockets and leaned back against the sofa, his thin body holding itself rigid to support the straight line from buttock to shoulder.

"It's okay, Grandad, really. Relax."

He looked at me, eyes wide. I turned back to the chess board, my eyes shifting over the pattern the pieces made, searching for whatever deep logic might be held there. I couldn't see it, although my eyes continued sweeping, memorising, looking for some rule or device. I felt my nose twitch, then the rest of my face. I felt I was staring at the answer I needed and it was written in a language I didn't yet understand. I tried to recall the movement, the sequence, the rhythm. I had watched him many times over many years, but without really seeing.

"Don't be angry, Jo. Don't be angry."

How did he do that? How did he tune in so accurately to what I was feeling? My body hadn't changed, or my expression. I was just staring at the chess board. I could force a laugh, turn and hug him, but he wouldn't be fooled. The only thing that would calm him was if I really became calm myself. And I couldn't do it. I hated that I wasn't master of my own emotions.

"What are you thinking about, Jo? What's making you angry?"

"I'm not really angry, just frustrated. I want to know why people need so much stuff, why they can't just be happy with less."

He nodded, looking seriously into my face.

"What do you think?"

"Me?"

Was it such a rare thing for me to ask for his opinion? I cursed my arrogance. "Yeah."

His expression compressed and then cleared. "It's because it's too easy. Because of money."

"What do you mean?"

"Because you can buy anything with money, and it comes straight away, people think that everything would be easy if they had more money. But it isn't. It takes effort to get things. Paying money just means other people do the work, not you."

I blinked, trying to unravel what he was saying.

"Like at the petrol station. Sometimes I think people would use less petrol if it didn't just flow out of the tanks into their cars. They don't have to do anything, just put the nozzle in and wait, like being in a lift." He closed his eyes. It was an old family legend. There were no lifts in Folkstown, and the first time he went in one, in Dunedin, in the hospital where my mother was born, he had thought he was going mad, then he thought it was magic – he got into a box, and when the doors reopened, the world had changed. He never got inside one again.

"How is it? How is it like being in a lift?" I was eager. Too eager. He looked at me nervously once more. I deliberately slowed my heart, reined in my impatience.

"Nothing seems to happen, you don't see anything happen. But the tank goes from empty to full, you can drive again. And all you have to do is pay. If people actually had to see the petrol, get it in a bucket and pour it into their cars, it would be real. Like walking up the stairs instead of taking the lift. They would know where they were."

For one insane second I opened my mouth to argue. It was just convenience. It didn't make sense to fill a car with petrol using a bucket. But luckily something rang in my head telling me to shut up, telling me I couldn't take this conversation at face value. There was another kind of logic here, something so simple that all my mind-training and education would have made me miss it. If I didn't love Grandad so much, I would have missed it.

I began to think I'd been missing things all my life, more and more and more as I became more sure of my genius and my superiority. The sentence clicked into a different perspective. It was just convenience.

Convenience was what was ruining the world.

SLOW TIME

8

My grandmother was a brilliant woman. Everybody said so. I had felt a little of it myself, in the few years I'd known her before she died. Her eyes were piercing; she saw things other people didn't see, because her mind worked so much faster. I recalled one conversation clearly. She had pulled me back from the road when I thought it was safe to cross. I had asked her why. Her answer was full of calculations, probability. She explained why it was better to cross a little further down the road.

I remember staring into her face, overcome with her beauty as she reeled off the numbers, euphoric in her world of rapid thought and understanding. I asked her more questions, forgetting my destination. We moved onto the bench behind us and sat like that for some time, discussing next the flight of birds, the interaction of a small flock nearby, pecking for food, rising in approximate unison off the ground, a pair of them chasing on the wing, their movement increasing in complexity exponentially as they reacted and responded to each other. I felt a great sense of expansion as this world of brilliance opened up to me, and a jolt of delight when she suddenly hugged me, a glint of tears in her eyes. "I think you're quite like me," she said. "I'm happy about that. It's such a relief."

I thought about those words for years after. What did she mean, a relief? Before I could ask her, she was gone, and then my mother. Dad just shook his head when I asked him, and I'd never thought of Grandad. Until now. But a more urgent question hovered. People often wondered aloud why she married him. What did a brilliant woman like her see in him? I had defended them both, tooth and nail, and never really considered the question myself. It seemed disloyal. She loved him. I knew that. But now I began to wonder, with intensity as if it held the answer to life, what it was. What did she see that everyone else missed; including me, who knew better than anyone how important it was to love him? I had taken him at face value for a shockingly long time.

"Grandad?"

"Yes, Love."

"I'm thinking about something. Can I tell you about it?"

He nodded, turning towards me, both feet planted on the floor as he sat on the sofa. Waiting. And now I couldn't think what I was going to say. He gave no sign of impatience, simply sat with his eyes calmly resting on my face. I felt peaceful, despite the disorder of my thoughts.

"I want to help. Everyone. I want to help the town.'

"I'm glad, Jo. I think you're the only one who can do it."

"Thanks. But I need to know if what I do is working. I need to know what things are like for people now. And I don't know how to find that out without seeming . . . impertinent, nosy. What do you think? Do you think I should call a meeting, tell them what I'm doing, ask for their help?"

"No."

I waited, too quickly becoming impatient again. "No, what?"

"No, I don't think you should do that."

"Then what? What should I do?"

"I think you should go to them one by one, ask them one by one."

"But what if they won't listen? What if they don't trust me?"

"You tell them. Tell them you want to help."

"You think they'll believe me?"

He frowned, confused. "Of course they'll believe you. It's true."

So simple. The difference between truth and lies. For someone who relies so much on words, like me, it's easy to forget the simple fact that there is a basic, tangible difference between truth and lies.

It took almost more courage than I possessed to go to the people I loved and respected and ask them to tell me about their failure. Josie was okay – she had already admitted defeat. Louise was another step up, and then there were the others, those who were still clinging to the fiction that everything would be okay.

Word began to spread around town before me, people started to look wary when I approached them, but with some veiled hope there, too. A miracle was beyond their comprehension just yet, clouded by their shifting, creeping fear. The downward slide was slow enough that they could make a conscious denial, even though in their hearts they knew it was real.

There was another hurdle to take, too, one I was putting off day by day. Surely it would have to wait till after Christmas, till after the vacation? Deep inside me, though, I knew it needed to be done soon. If this was to be my dissertation, my first contribution to the world's body of knowledge, I needed to find a supervisor, and work out some direction before I went too far. I woke up one morning knowing it had to be today.

9

It made sense to phone ahead, make appointments, see who was around. But my gut said, no. Just go there. It will all work out.

"Dad, can I borrow your car today? I need to go to Christchurch."

He looked up at me over his cereal, then glanced at Grandad. His eyebrows flexed. There was a pause. "Sure."

"You won't need it?"

"I had some things I was going to do today. They'll wait."

I breathed a deep inhale and out again. Every little obstacle these days had me holding my breath, waiting, like it was life or death. "Thanks. I'll be back for dinner. Don't wait if I'm a little late."

I found a good jacket in the wardrobe, left there after a wedding last summer, and put it on quickly, before I could change my mind. I looked at my notes, lying across my bedroom floor. It made sense to take them, but I knew the detail would only distract. It was the big picture I needed to present today. I picked up my backpack, saggy with only my wallet and a notebook inside.

"See you later."

It was seven thirty, and the light was still slanting across the landscape, the shadows highlighting the contours of the hills. Later, when the sun was high, they would lose their definition. I preferred the contrast, darkness emphasising the beauty of the light. My mind roved over this metaphor, beauty only visible through light; and beyond that, the observer essential to witness it, to make it real. How far could I take this, and was I only justifying myself, aggrandising myself, making out nobility in what I wanted, when maybe what I really wanted was recognition, someone to see me clearly?

If my plan worked, the town might thank me, or it might not. Perhaps once this was successful, my credit for it would be lost. Was that why I wanted to do it this way? I told myself that by writing it up, others would have access to it, so they could learn from it and use it, too. That was undeniably true. But did some part of me crave the credit? Was I looking for immortality? And if I were, was that wrong?

I turned away from the painful soul-searching, but Highway 72 is a long straight road, and I couldn't evade my thoughts for long.

The conversation was efficient, brief, disproportionately encouraging. The professor who was my first choice was in her office, free to talk and immediately captivated by the idea.

"It's inspiring. A real-life story. The saving of a town! I can't think of anything more worthy." Leonie's eyes were alight.

My lower lip wobbled. I hadn't realised how alone I had felt, how lonely. I put my hand to my face, squeezed my nose, wiped my mouth to stop myself crying.

"Now, details. You know these people, they're willing to talk to you?"

I nodded, holding back the flood of history. A simple answer was all that was required.

"So what information are you gathering?"

I told her, received her suggestions gratefully. I was on the right track, which was a relief to hear even though I knew it already, and her insights allowed me to expand my vision, look further than I had before.

"And what do you know about Slow Time, about the movement? You've read Honoré's book, you said."

"And I've done some internet research. There are several towns around the world who have signed the manifesto. Each one is different. Not everything will work here, or work towards what we want to achieve. I don't think any of the other towns were struggling before taking this on. I think they were mostly looking for improvement in quality of life, rather than the saving of it. This is a new experiment."

She nodded. "We'll need to get you some grant money so you can travel, see what's been done elsewhere."

My head jerked up. "Really?"

She smiled. "Really."

"But I didn't . . . this isn't about me. I don't need perks. I just want to do the best for the people I love."

Her smile twisted into an expression of surprise. "Is there something you haven't told me?"

My head shook, side to side. "No. I don't think so."

"Well, then. Take a step back. Look at it logically. Don't you think it would help?"

I stared out her window at the corners of other buildings, the tops of the tallest trees. I felt a sense of panic, of urgency. The thought of leaving, of going away for any length of time scared me.

"I'm worried about what will happen if I'm not there."

Her eyes narrowed. "You think everything will collapse without you?"

"I know it's not logical . . ."

"It's also not healthy. You need some perspective, objectivity. If you get in too close you won't be able to see clearly."

"But I need to be involved. This is my vision. I need to be in there to make it work."

"It will be a fine line. Or perhaps rather you need a dual perspective. Be both observer and observed. Can you do that?"

"I don't know." I closed my eyes, trying to feel my way to an answer. I heard her take a deep breath through her nose.

"Well. I'm sure you can." My eyes flicked open to see the end of her decisive nod. I grasped it like a lifeline, took her words as creative declaration. I could. I would. She pulled some papers towards her and I took my cue to leave.

"Thank you," I said, as I stood up.

Her mind was already on her next task. "Send me your proposal, by next week if possible. And keep in touch." She glanced up, focused on me briefly once more. "I mean it. I'm here at the end of the phone when things get tough."

I nodded again. I was more grateful than I could express, and more scared than I dared say out loud.

This drive would become my sanity, I could see that already. I started back with my breath short, coming in too-shallow spasms, following one another after too-long pauses. Perhaps I should have stopped for a coffee in the student union caff, but I needed to be on my own. Once on the open road I felt calmer. It was still only early afternoon and the traffic was light. I fell in gratefully behind a farmer in a hat travelling at ninety, allowing faster cars to pass us both on the passing lanes. After Rakaia it was even easier, there was no traffic at all. I remembered the cassette player, looked in the glove-box and found a battered copy of Mozart's Requiem, the soaring, shifting harmony exactly what I needed to calm my restless mind. This was too much. I was too small. I couldn't do it . . . and there was no-one else. It was all up to me. I had to do it.

I dwelt on this idea for a long time, feeling another rise and fall of terror and expansion. Once the fog of fear cleared into the open view of necessity, it all looked easier, possible. There was no-one else to do it, therefore there was nothing to lose. I would give it my best shot; maybe I would die trying; but there truly was nothing to lose.

SLOW TIME

10

I woke to a new optimism. Caroline was arriving today, bringing my suitcases, my books. I could have made a side trip yesterday and picked them up, but I needed to focus on one thing at a time. Besides, I wanted to see her. She was going to stay over. I had pulled the old mattress out from under my bed, made it up with the best sheets, the warmest blankets. For twenty-four hours I could relax in the company of someone who expected nothing from me. Bliss.

She breezed in about ten, long brown hair lifting slightly in the light wind.

"Hey, Babe, good to see you. Did you miss me?"

"You have no idea." I hugged her, clinging for a second then forcing myself to let go before I freaked her out. She held on to me, looking into my face.

"Hey, steady! You okay?"

I grinned. "Yeah. Sure. I am just SO glad to see you."

"Tired of wearing the same sweatshirt, the same jeans?" She walked around to the back of her car and opened the boot.

"Yeah, that, too."

"Come on, help me with this. What have you got in here? Bricks?"

"Oh, you know. Books."

"But I know you own clothes, I've seen them. Where are they?"

"Wrapped around the books." I smirked apologetically and helped her haul the bag over the lip of the boot. Once on the ground there were wheels to make it more manageable. We both laughed as it moved of its own accord, accelerating quickly and tipping over into the gutter.

"Grab it, it's trying to make a break for it!"

"The other one?"

"I've got it. Come on, I'm dying for a coffee. We can get the rest later."

I left the suitcase I was wheeling in the hall and headed straight for the kitchen. "Coffee here? Or do you want to go out?" I heard the hysterical rising note in my voice.

Caroline took the cafetière out of my hand and put it back on the counter. "Okay. You're not fooling anyone. What is it? Spill."

I put my hands on the edge of the bench and gripped hard. "I've been holding so much in. I don't want to kill you in the avalanche." I turned to face her. "Seriously, let me get the coffee, get used to the fact that you're here, and I'll get everything in some sort of order before it comes tumbling out in a mess."

"Let it tumble. I don't care."

I shook my head. "You said you wanted coffee." I was holding on. Holding on. But my grip was slipping.

"Okay. We're fixated on the coffee." She pointed to the bar stool in the corner of the little kitchen. "Go over there. Start talking. I'll do this."

I hesitated. She reached past me for the kettle, put it under the tap to fill and pointed to the stool again with the other hand. I felt something inside me relax, slumping into a heap. It was such a relief to have someone tell me what to do for a change. I backed towards the bar stool and hefted myself up onto it.

"Now start talking."

"I don't know where to begin."

"You were going home to get some rest. How did that go?"

I laughed, recalling my first hours here, and began the story.

I felt the joy of having an eager, compassionate audience, of being truly understood. Caro got the nuance without me spelling it out. Bald facts came to life reflected in her face.

"God! Oh, God! But if anyone can do it, you can."

I laughed, relaxation sounding through my whole body.

"And if I can't?"

"Then like you said, you'll die trying. You're actually lucky. A lot of people would give anything to be so needed, and so loved."

"So loved." I repeated the expression experimentally.

"Yeah. That's what it is, isn't it? That's where the pressure comes in. But it's a good thing, too. A really good thing."

"I guess."

"Don't guess, know!"

"How?"

"Like I do with Mikey . . ."

"But you know you love him, you're like chips and dip, burger and cheese, hot dog and mustard."

"No. Not always. Sometimes I look at him and I feel like I'm going to explode. But you know why I never throw him out?"

"Okay, I'll play along. Why?"

"I think what life would be like without him. If he left, how would I feel? And I know I'd do anything, anything to get him back."

"And the moral of the story . . ?"

"How would you feel if you didn't matter here? If no-one knew you or cared? If no-one depended on you."

I considered her words, and it was like a chasm opening up. "I can't imagine. I wouldn't know what to do. If I didn't have home to come to . . . how would I live?"

"So that's how lucky you are. Some people only have one or two people who care this much about them. And some people have no-one at all."

At that moment, something clicked into place inside me, deep certainty, a deep awareness of privilege. I'd been holding back, resisting. No more.

First, though, we'd have a day of celebration, a day of rest before returning to the fray.

"Okay. I got it. Thanks."

"Anytime. So what now?"

"Let's go out on the town. Get a DVD. Come back and chill."

11

We walked slowly, laughing, talking. We never run out of things to talk about. Sometimes when we're apart I wonder how we do it, and I think it's that we cover the same ground, each time deeper, over and over again. I work out my theories about life with Caroline, and she does with me. I can say something, start to get at something, get it wrong and try again. It's so liberating. In the echoing chamber of my own mind things don't work out so fast. I can think things through a certain way, but then they just go round and round with very little progress.

"So what do you think about this Slow Time? What is it, really?"

"I don't know. I've been thinking. It's not just about slowing down. It's about what happens when you do slow down. What I think is that, at a slower pace, priorities shift. Things that seem important when you're rushing just aren't when you have time. Grandad said it first. Convenience is so important when you're trying to pack more and more in. But maybe it doesn't have any value at all by itself."

"But there are things that need to be done, surely. Like cooking and washing up and washing clothes. It makes sense to have those done so you can focus on more important things."

"Maybe. Maybe not. I think we've forgotten how to contemplate. The modern thing is to meditate: quiet room, nothing happening, stare into a flame. But maybe the same result is better obtained through the hypnotic repetition of daily tasks. And maybe we eat better if we've been in touch with the food beforehand."

Caroline's eyes widened as she tried to take this in, as if she'd tried to swallow too big a bite of something.

"I don't know if I'm right. It's just the start of an idea. Slowing down means you see different patterns."

"Patterns?"

"I know. It's all so half-baked. But you know how a different perspective can totally alter things. Speed creates illusions like a spinning fan looks like a circle . . . oh, I give up! I sound crazy."

Caroline put an arm around me. "Einstein sounded crazy. Edison. Galileo. What do the other Slow Timers say?"

"I don't know. I haven't found anything that seems to get to the heart of it. Everything I've read seems to be about running away from something. It all talks about reducing stress, reducing rush, getting back to better health. But there's no forward vision, no big picture of something new."

"So you're going to have to come up with one."

"Yeah. I guess. On top of everything else." Suddenly I felt tired again. I had got excited, inspired, while I followed the path of my new thoughts as they bounced off Caroline, freshened and clarified.

"Relax. Give it time. Think about it while you do the washing up."

I hit her, quite hard, on the shoulder. "Won't you shut up feeding my own bullshit back to me."

She feigned upset. "Aw, Jo, don't be mean."

Dinner was fun. Dad and Grandad love Caroline nearly as much as I do. Her family had lived here till she was fourteen, until they had made their fortune and took it to Wanaka for the billionaires' lifestyle at millionaires' prices. For all the money she's very down to earth.

Grandad's smile grew wider and wider as he turned from me to Caro and back again. "It's good to have you here," he repeated, over and over again.

After dinner Dad and I did the washing up. Grandad wanted to help, to give me more time with Caroline, but she convinced him I really wanted to do it. "It's good for her. Helps her get perspective." I wanted to hit her again, but watched them fondly back into the living room. Everyone loves Grandad, but Caroline really knows how to listen to him. I hadn't noticed that before.

Dad washed and I dried without talking. Ten minutes went by.

"You're very quiet," he said, finally.

"Yeah."

"Everything good?"

"Yeah. You?"

He nodded. "I had a good day." The lines between his eyes creased for a moment, then disappeared again. "Something's changing."

"Yeah. I know. I feel it, too."

"Know what it is?"

"Not yet. But I'm getting there. I think we can trust it."

"Yeah. Yeah. I think so, too. Dad's right. It's good having Caro here. It's good to see you laugh again."

I frowned, sharply. "Had I stopped laughing?"

He held up his hands. When had I got so touchy? "No criticism. Things have been hard."

"Well, maybe it's time they got easy." And there it was. That was it. That was the answer.

Caro and I laughed like schoolgirls late into the night. I had to force myself to stop talking. She had a big drive tomorrow, she needed her sleep. I leaned down and ruffled her hair.

"What do you want, Caroline?"

"I want love and a long life and happiness."

"Tell me what that looks like."

And she started talking, filling in the details, growing wilder and wilder in her kaleidoscopic visions. My 'mm's and 'aha's gradually faded away and we both fell asleep to the magic of her dreams.

I helped Caro carry her stuff out to the car, carefully arranging her bags around the box of vegetables Grandad had picked her from his garden. I didn't want to let her go – it felt like the holidays were over, like waking up on Monday morning with too much work to do.

"What is it?"

"Nothing . . . just wondering if I'm really up to this."

"You are . . . and . . ."

"What?"

"I have a question . . ."

"Yes? What? What is it?"

"Patience! Jeesh! I was just wondering, why the Slow thing? There are a million ways you could revitalise the town. Probably easier ways. Why this?"

"I don't know. It just sort of feels right."

"Well then . . ."

"What? Come on! Spit it out!"

She laughed then, right out loud.

"What!"

"I just think you might want to ease into this a bit. Let it sit. I think there might be more to this than you realise. I don't think you can hurry becoming Slow."

I tossed my head. "I know that!"

She screwed up her face in that maddening, pretty way she has. "You see, there it is, right there. Patience has never really been your thing, has it?"

"So. So I'm not perfect. So what?" I peered into her face as she continued laughing at me. "Ah . . ." And then I began to laugh, too, at myself.

"I'll see you at New Year, yeah?"

"Yeah. Can't wait."

SLOW TIME

12

We never let Grandad wash the dishes – he dried, but never washed. It was a habit with a long-forgotten beginning. Today I made a change, just to see what would happen.

I took the tea towel from him where he waited, quite still, for the first dish. "Why don't you wash? I'll dry."

I felt guilty as I watched his face light up. He stepped past me to the sink and looked at the plug for a minute before gently easing it into the hole. He spent a few minutes arranging the dishes into washing order: glasses nearest the sink, then plates, then cutlery, which he put in a bowl to soak, then the pots and pans. I stilled my tapping foot, forcing myself to pay attention to his movements, understand the logic. It was ten minutes before the first glass was clean and draining, soapy water forming bubbles which popped and fizzed in the heat seal underneath it. I picked it up.

"Not yet, Jo. Wash first, then rinse. Otherwise it'll taste bad."

I shifted my weight onto my other foot, biting back my words. I couldn't see how it would work. Watch and learn, I told myself. Watch and learn.

Once the glasses were all stacked and clean on the drainer, he turned on the tap again, just a trickle, and held each glass under the stream, tilting it this way and that till all the bubbles were gone. Finally he held out his perfect finished product. I took it and quickly dried it, opening the cupboard and putting it inside with a sharp thunk. Then I waited for the next one. After two or three more I realised something else was happening. He wasn't just rinsing the glasses, he was playing with the light, dancing the refracted highlights over the other glasses, the taps, up onto the window. I opened my mouth to comment, then closed it. Watch.

The pause between pieces was driving me crazy, especially as I forbad my foot to tap or my fingers to gallop. I tried to slow my breath, find something else to occupy me, but I felt like I was going to hop out of my skin. Caro was right: this wasn't going to be easy. I let my thoughts wander, contemplating the wider implications of Slow. Just this tiny piece I hadn't understood. How much more was there? One thing, for sure, next time I wouldn't have that second cup of coffee with dinner. Held still from their jittering, I felt my fingers literally vibrate to dissipate the nervous energy. I reached past Grandad to run water into a newly clean, dry glass, taking a quick gulp, then a few slower sips. He was right, it did taste better. How many years had he known this, yet never complained?

My thoughts slipped back into impatience. Maybe I could tidy the living room a little, come back when there was a bit of a backlog to dry. No. Stop. This is it. This is the moment. You'll either get this, now, or you're kidding yourself. Get this now, or the whole idea will fall apart. I closed my eyes and took a deep breath. Slow. Slow. God, I don't know if I can do this.

"This is nice. Amelia always let me wash, too."

I shook myself out of my thoughts. "Really?"

He smiled into the soapy water. "It was my favourite time of the day. Fed, feeling good. Kids bathed and ready for bed, all the work done."

"Tell me about Grandma. I remember her, but . . ."

"She was a good woman. A good woman."

I waited, reining in my impatience once more. It was easier this time. I sensed the words would be different if I didn't hurry him. That if I really listened he would have more to say.

"She was like you in lots of ways - quick, clever." He said it proudly, but I wasn't feeling so proud of this aspect of myself just now. "People said she could have gone away, she could have done anything. But she loved it here." He shook his head, left to right, once. "I could never think of being anywhere else, but I would have gone, if she'd wanted. I even could have got used to those lifts." He glanced at me out of the corner of his eye. I couldn't tell if he was laughing at me or at himself. "And she was ambitious. But she liked home, too, family. She loved the children. Your mum. I'm glad she wasn't here when your mum went. She couldn't have borne it." His face was stricken now. Somehow it had never hit me before that Mum was his daughter, too. He had always seemed more like her child than the other way around. I'd never thought of him having a parent's grief. He handed me a plate and I dried it, tears rolling down my face. I wiped them with my arm.

"It must have been hard for you, facing that on your own."

He shook his head again. "I never really feel alone."

"You've got Dad. And me."

His eyes squinted briefly. "Yes . . . but . . ."

"What?" Shut up. Wait. My toe lifted automatically. I caught it and put it down gently.

He looked off into the distance, but he couldn't have seen anything in the present, sunlight was streaming in the window, illuminating his face, blinding him. A rueful smile touched his mouth, crept upwards towards his eyes. In a movement that startled me he turned towards me, focusing on my face. "I hear her, you know." He said it daringly. "She talks to me. Tells me what to do." His words hung there, between us. He watched me carefully for my reaction, and I carefully considered what it would be. I thought my face was blank. "I'm not, you know."

"Not what?"

"Not crazy."

The words had flickered through my mind, but I hadn't said them. "I know you're not."

His face fell and he looked back into the water again. "Amelia understood me."

"I know, Grandad. I'm trying. I really am."

He looked up again, hopeful.

"I'll get there, in the end, if you give me time."

"Course I will, Love. Thanks." He handed me another plate. I dried it slower this time.

13

In my dreams I struggled with the bigger picture. How could I convince the town to a new way of life when I couldn't master the simplest rudiments of it myself? I lay in bed hating the ceiling. What the hell! Do something practical.

Louise had decided to sell her house, to pay off her debts. I wasn't sure it was the right thing to do. With more people leaving than arriving, property values weren't high.

She and Jason lived in one of the grand old houses, rambling and gorgeous, seven bedrooms, three living rooms, ancient, unreliable plumbing and wiring, attics full of the relics of three generations. The garden needed clearing before it went on the market. I'd throw myself into that today, take a break from everything else.

She came out onto the porch with her thin dressing gown pulled tight around her. "What time is it?"

I looked up guiltily. "It's after six."

She squeezed one eye tight shut, opening the other wider. "Six."

"I couldn't sleep. I thought I'd make a start."

She turned back towards the door. "I'll make us a cup of tea."

Louise sat on the porch steps, her hands warming against her mug, long after I had drained mine and returned to work. "It's going to be a good day."

I looked up at the sky, became conscious of the balmy air. "Yeah." I bit back my many questions. What was she planning for herself today? Had they started painting inside yet? Up till a couple of years ago, when the café was doing well, the house had been fairly well maintained, but there were a couple of formal living areas which the family didn't use much, which were a little tired.

"The agent thinks we'll get around $400,000, if we can find a buyer."

"Did she say how likely that was?"

"Oh, you know, it's her job to be optimistic."

"And? Was she?"

"Well, no, to be honest. But it's worth a try."

"Is it?"

She glared at me, finally waking up properly.

"This is your family home. I don't think you should sell it. Not now, anyway."

"So you've said. But what choice do I have? I can't make my loan payments, let alone eat as well."

"We won't let you go hungry. You know that."

"I don't like charity."

"Oh, for Pete's sake."

"Don't talk to me like that."

I straightened up, taking off the gardening gloves I had borrowed from Dad's work bag. I was angry. I had just wanted a day off from worrying, from thinking all the time. "Get a grip on yourself, Louise. Fight back."

"I am, you nasty little toe rag. I knew you when you were, God, not even thought of, what makes you think you can treat me like I'm worthless?"

"I don't think you're worthless. Spineless, maybe."

She put her mug down on the step next to her. Her shoulders widened. She walked slowly down the steps and across the lawn to stand directly in front of me. We stared into each other's eyes for a moment, then before I even saw it coming I felt the hard slap of her hand on my cheek. Tears came to my eyes, and hers. "You just have no idea. You come back from your coddled little university life, queen of the world, and you dare to judge me. You have no right. No right."

I felt my chest shake, jerking sobs shaking out of me. "Where did you go, Louise? You're supposed to be the grown-up. I can't do this on my own."

"Well, if you want every little thing done your own little way, you're going to have to. Either that or let people make their own choices in their own way. I'm going to sell my house, I'm going to pay my way and I'm going to keep my dignity. To hell with your judgement. You can help if you want, but ask first, don't just turn up, and never tell me what to do again."

I hesitated then. Was she telling me to go? I looked down at the pile of pulled weeds at my feet. Bizarrely I felt I couldn't leave until I had cleared them away, put them in the burner or at least in a tidy heap somewhere. I waved at them vaguely. "Do you want me to go?" I felt so tiny, like I was five, or six, and I'd spilled my juice on the café floor. "Let me clear this up first."

But then her arms were around me, pulling me close, stroking my hair. "You want me to be the grown-up, then let me be the grown-up. You know I love you, even when I'm going mad."

I clutched onto the blue satin, my grip too much for it. "I'm sorry."

"That's okay, Hon. We're all a little stressed. I'll go have a shower, get some breakfast, then you can come inside and tell me what you think I can do if I don't sell. That bed and breakfast idea. Convince me it could work, and maybe I can listen now."

I watched her up the steps, her once perfect hair blowsy and frayed. I wished my mother were here, for both of us.

14

Another cup of tea, another go at getting this right.

"This house, it's perfect. It's just the sort of place people want to stay."

"There's too much work to be done. The front rooms need painting and there are only two bathrooms that actually work."

"Well, maybe that's enough to start. And the painting's easy. I can do it myself. It'll be a relief to do something I can actually get more or less right."

"But how will it work? I don't see how it will work."

"You don't have to. I do. How much do you need each month to pay the bills?"

"Just over $1,000 for the loan. Maybe another $1,000 for me and Jason to live, to eat, to pay the power and the phone."

"Well, that's got to be easy. I need some income, what say you take the first $2,000 profit each month, and then we split the rest, 80:20. I'll set it up, do the marketing. You just have to be here, greet the guests, show them their rooms, make them breakfast. When you need time off, you call me. Please. Say yes."

Her chest twitched in the tiniest laugh. "All right. All right. I give up. We'll try it. A few months."

I felt my face creak into a smile. It hurt. "Okay. Show me the house, everything, so I can work out what needs to be done."

The master bedroom had an en-suite, so that was easy: that would be the first room. The second bathroom wasn't so simple, it was down the hall from the nearest bedroom, then there were two bedrooms, one of them Jason's, that came off the same landing so it wasn't easily separated off. "Let me think about this. I'm sure there's a way."

"And what are Jason and I going to do? Wash in the stream out back?"

"Both rooms won't be full all the time. You can use whichever's free – don't look at me like that, I know it's not ideal."

"And when they are both occupied?"

"I said let me think about it. Give me time."

We carried on the tour. There were four more bedrooms, a large landing around the central staircase, and the downstairs parlours, kitchen, laundry and downstairs toilet. "Breakfast room, guest lounge and family living. Easy. We'll put a dining table in the kitchen for you and Jason. And there's room in the laundry for a shower. You can use that when it's full upstairs. Dad can put one in this weekend. Easy."

Louise wrinkled her nose.

"What?"

"Nothing. I just hate admitting you're right."

"Well, then, don't. We'll just pretend it was all your idea."

"And what about the furniture in the front rooms? It will need to be replaced."

"Nah, faded grandeur, people love it. A few throws and cushions and it'll be fine. We need to move it out so I can paint, though, I'm a menace with a roller."

"But there's no rush for that, is there?"

"Sure there is. I want to start this afternoon."

"What happened to Slow Time?"

"Shut up. I'll be contemplating while I paint. Besides, didn't you say you had a loan payment due next week?"

"Yeah. But there's no way we'll make that. I'll go down, talk to the bank again."

"Not yet. Just hold off a couple of days. Who knows?"

We dragged Jason out of bed, moved everything from one front room into the other. I stood turning in the space, working out how much paint we needed, deciding we could get away without doing the ceiling or the woodwork. "It's not perfect but it will do. Once the big wall areas are painted it will look fine."

I borrowed Louise's car to pick up the paint and stopped on the way at the tourist information centre.

"Hey Kathy! How are you?"

"Little Jo! How lovely to see you. I heard you were home. Not staying up in the big city for the holidays?"

"No, I'm here for a while. That's why I came to see you. I'm going to be working with Louise, see about making her house a bed and breakfast. We'll have a couple of rooms ready by the weekend. Just need you to send us some guests." It sounded half-baked as it came out of my mouth, but Kathy didn't seem at all surprised.

"I've always thought that house could be something. Will you have some brochures?"

"We will, but not yet. But can you tell people about us in the meantime? They can always drive past and have a look. Here's Louise's phone number, and my mobile. And will you tell the others as well?"

Kathy smiled that familiar, indulgent smile, the one all my adopted mothers used when I was on another hare-brained scheme. It used to drive me crazy, but I was grateful for it now. She nodded. "From Friday, you said?"

"From Friday." I crossed my fingers behind my back. I wouldn't tell Louise just yet, wait till I'd finished painting one room, got a couple of beds made up.

Next stop was the hardware store. I used to work here, the last year before I left for university. "Hi, Pete."

"Hey! Need some more information for that project of yours?"

"Not just at the moment. Thanks, though, I'll come and see you soon. Right now I need a bigger favour."

I felt awful, asking for credit when I knew how tight things were. With luck, though, I'd have paid him within the month, and at least it was a sale for him. He agreed without blinking. I grinned. "You're an angel! Dad will pick up the shower on Saturday, I think. I'll take the paint now."

"Okay. How much, and what colour?"

I picked out a light neutral shade from the chart, something that would stand back and let the architecture of the house speak.

"Need undercoat?"

"Yeah, that wallpaper's pretty vivid."

He put in some filler, sandpaper, drop sheets, brushes and rollers and rang it up with a big discount. I shook my head. "No, Pete. I want to pay the going rate. When I can."

"When you can we'll talk about it. In the meantime this is fine."

I hugged him. He blushed.

"You know what you're doing with all this?"

"Think so. How hard can it be?"

He laughed. "Maybe I'll drop by later and check on you."

SLOW TIME

15

I started work straight away, filling gaps, sanding. My Slow Time mantra repeated in my head as I worked. Images of the rooms upstairs turned around and around. I was excited about arranging them.

Through the window I saw Louise continuing with the garden clearing I had abandoned. Good. Jason returned from a run and hovered in the hallway until I threw him a paintbrush. I showed him how to cut in: below the picture rail, over the skirting board, around the doors and windows.

"Where did you learn this?"

"Grandad taught me. We did my room together when I was ten."

"And you remember?"

"It seemed pretty easy. I'll work it out."

I read the side of the filler pot. "Leave to dry at least an hour before painting." It was a warm day, and the windows were open, but still there was a gap of time before Jason could finish edging and we could roll. I looked up, tilting my head speculatively.

"Come with me. I have an idea."

He followed obediently. "What is it?" he asked, as we ascended the stairs.

"How would you feel about moving out of your room?" We stood in the hall. "See the problem we have? To get top rates the rooms need to have en-suites, but the best bathroom doesn't share a wall with a bedroom. What if we take these two bedrooms, make one of them a living room and turn this into a suite? All we'd have to do is put a door in here. We could charge way more for it." I tilted my head on one side, trying to look beguiling.

"Stop that. It won't work." But he was grinning.

"You don't mind moving?"

"Guess not, if it means we can stay in the house. I'd have to move out if we sold it, right?"

"Right. Good way of looking at it. So which room do you want? I'll help you shift."

"You're the boss, which room can I have?"

I screwed my face up at him. "Let's look together, shall we?"

It felt so good to be doing something. Jason's things went into one of the smaller rooms with a view over the garden, and we took two small sofas out of two bedrooms and put them in his old room. With cushions scavenged from various rooms and a couple of occasional tables, it looked quite inviting. We moved around a few paintings and stood back to look. "Fine."

"Yeah. Cool."

Next was the bedroom opposite. It had a good brass bedstead but the bedding was vivid and awful. "Is there anything else?"

We hunted through the linen cupboard, finding, right at the bottom, a stack of beautiful old lace sheets. "Do you think we could use these?" I whispered. "They look like antiques."

"I'll ask Mum."

Louise came inside. "What are you two doing, ransacking the place?"

I showed her the new sitting room, explained the idea of the suite. "The lace would be perfect. Can we?"

"Yes. Sure. They were my mother's. She never used them. A bit of a waste. We'll just have to be careful how we wash them. But beautiful things should be used."

We went back downstairs. The filler was dry now and I sanded it before taking over the paintbrush from Jason. "You can use the roller. Be grateful, it's a big sacrifice, my favourite job."

Our industry seemed to work like a magnet. Dad turned up an hour later having finished his work for the day. I showed him the laundry. "Do you think you can put the shower in this weekend?"

"Why wait? I'll do it now."

We looked at the upstairs hall, too. He turned to Louise. "You happy about this little upstart turning your house upside down?"

"No, I'm not." She stuck out her tongue at me, and I reciprocated. "But it's that or sell. She still hasn't explained how I'm going to pay for it, though, that's a bit of a worry."

"You'll do your bit for free, won't you, Dad?"

"If you say so."

"And I've got a deal going with Pete. So don't worry."

" 'Don't worry', she says. Right."

It felt good working with Dad's bangs, crashes and swearing going on at the other end of the house. Jason left once he finished rolling, but Grandad turned up after work to help Louise in the garden. There was something here, something about us all working together. I needed to get the town pulled together, just like this. But it felt too desperate. So many of them were hurting, struggling, and trying to pretend they weren't. Think, come on, think! There must be a way of overcoming that.

Dad seemed to have it right, slowing things down, offering hospitality, food, a place to sit around and yarn with old friends. Around six he came through, dusty, tired and grinning. "That'll do today. I'll fix up what I haven't worked out yet tomorrow. You ready for tea? Louise is coming, and I called Josie, too."

I looked around the room. I was nearly finished cutting in the first top coat. It looked bad, the new colour muddy and uneven against the white of the undercoat. I knew it would come out all right, but it was discouraging at this point. "Let me finish the edges so I can roll first thing tomorrow. I'll be there in half an hour?"

The others left, their warm voices fading down the path. Bring people together. But first they had to have their basic needs met. Money worries needed to be forgotten, at least temporarily. I'd been a poor student, stretching my finances from week to week. Surely I could think of something.

I watched the regular spread and lift of the brush as I smoothed on the paint, back and forth, back and forth, skimming the edge of the windows, flicking against the corners where the roller wouldn't reach. I sat on the floor to line the skirting, stretching out to almost lying to reach as far as I could from one spot. Pride. That was something to consider. Necessity and pride and community. There must be some way to bring those things into line, to give us a base, a starting point, a place to be happy and create from.

I washed out the brush, taking far longer than necessary, watching the flow of paint and water, swirling and contorting and disappearing drain-wards from an apparently infinite source. Look for the pattern. Look for the pattern. I know the answer is here, somewhere, close, right in front of me. Just find it.

My mood stayed the same as I walked home, stepped through the doorway into warmth and light and the sound of familiar voices. I found a perch on the end of the sofa, ate my bread and stew and served up ice-cream for dessert, responding automatically to the friendly banter. Slow Time. Community. Slow Time. Community. Happy people. Creativity. It must be easy.

We waved goodbye to our guests around ten. I hugged Dad without words, kissed Grandad on the cheek and found my bed. It had been a long day, a good day. My breathing was deep and regular. I felt a fundamental confidence warming me as I drifted off to sleep.

I slept well till about four, but after I woke and fetched a glass of water, my dreams became chaotic. Over the last week they had been getting progressively more bizarre, but this was something else again.

I saw a line of people dressed in prison clothes, chained together at the ankles, shuffling forward towards me. I was scared at first, I didn't know what they wanted, but then I saw they had masks on their faces – smiling, happy masks. It's all right, I thought, but then I saw the eyes behind the masks were crying, and they had empty tin plates in their hands.

The next moment I was in a Victorian music hall, with underweight dancers doing the can-can, singing songs from the musical *Oliver*.

I woke in a sweat, the grey light of dawn more eerie than darkness. What did it mean? I tried to roll over and go back to sleep, but that wasn't happening. Instead I sat up, turned on the light and reached for my journal. I'd write it down. Maybe then I could sleep again. But as usual, once I got my pen in my hand, optimism took over. I wrote and wrote and wrote, about the dream, my feelings, my hopes and my fears. "This dream means something," I wrote. "What is it?"

Louise appeared in the doorway, sleepy and exasperated once again. "First gardening, now painting! It's six thirty. And don't you knock any more?"

"I didn't want to wake you, and I was up . . . you know . . ."

"Want some breakfast?"

"Yeah, that'd be great."

"I'll bring you some toast."

One wall was finished now and we sat looking at it as we ate.

"It's going to be good." She gestured up at the wall, then around the room.

"It sure is."

"It feels different already. I guess we'd got a little . . . stagnant."

"It's not surprising."

"I feel bad, though. You must have other things you should be doing."

I looked up into the corner of the room, searching for an answer. "I'm beginning to think the most direct route isn't always the fastest way. I kind of know where I'm going, but step-by-step isn't going to get me there. There are things that need to be dealt with first."

"Like what?"

"Like . . . well, like I've got an idea that I think could work for the whole town. But no-one's in a state to hear it. There's a lot of first aid that needs to happen, people need to be well fed and confident before they can take on a novel idea. But we can't just feed them. Even if we could, charity is not a way to make people feel better in the long term. And I . . . oh, forget it, it's so half-baked. I'll get back to you once I've worked it out."

"You want to feed them so you can bring them together?"

"Yeah, I guess that sums it up, metaphorically if not literally."

"Well, could you try it the other way around? Bring them together so you can feed them."

I stared at her. It was like she had handed me a piece of a jigsaw puzzle and I had no idea how to make it fit. But I knew it would fit, somehow. "Where? How? Our place is near overflowing with just the little group we had last night."

"My café's empty, doing nothing."

"So it is."

SLOW TIME

16

Ancient tribes would have gathered together to eat. This was the vague idea I had in mind as I stood looking at Louise's café with my father, working out how we could feed large numbers at low cost.

"You really are crazy, you know that?" Dad's expression was fond and annoyed. That didn't worry me unduly. He'd do what I wanted, because people always did in the end.

"Yeah. I do. But historically the crazy people were often also the visionaries."

"And there wouldn't be any delusions of grandeur?"

"Grandeur, prescience, immortality, calling. You name it. I'll need them all if I'm going to see this through."

"And are you? Are you going to stay, go the distance? You're not known for your long attention span. Are you going to leave us all in the lurch?"

It was a fair question. "No, Dad, I don't think so." My voice was low, lacking conviction. I cleared my throat before I continued. "Here. Help me rearrange these chairs. I want people to hang around after they've eaten, talk, tell stories, practise crafts. I've talked to Katrina, from the wool shop; she's going to set up a stall to sell wool, needles, so people can knit."

"Now I've heard everything!"

"Shut up! Trust me, I know what I'm doing."

"And you think knitting is going to save us?"

"Not by itself, Dad. Not by itself."

He brought in his slow-cooker, and called some of his mates whom he'd also converted. "I can cook for about ten in mine, especially if we have bread as well. We can do steamed vegetables in the microwave."

"Bit high tech, don't you think?"

"Slow Food is not about being reactionary. It's about quality. And microwaves do vegetables very well."

I left him filling the cooker and went back to work. One more top coat and we could move the furniture back in and start on the other room. I'd rather take more time, but . . . my thoughts stopped. I got it. If I'd rather take more time, I'd take it. Slow Time. Take all the time I need.

And the irony was, that even though I moved into a sort of slow motion, a state of timelessness, floating free, it still got done. I still finished the last top coat that afternoon, we still moved the furniture back before dinner. I even got the filling done on the other parlour so it could dry overnight. I was laughing, triumphant, almost shouting my breakthrough, and I couldn't make people understand.

"I didn't rush and it was even faster. Slow Time can be faster. It doesn't need to be, that's the point, and then it is because it doesn't need to be. You tap into something new."

"That's great, Jo. Really. Now calm down and have something to eat."

"I am calm. I am."

Several people laughed at this. Josie handed me her knitting. "Prove it. Let's see you do a row."

I put it down beside me. "Not now. Let me finish talking." More laughter. "I've just realised, it's not a pace, it's a state of mind. It's about knowing something matters, that it's important. It's about knowing why you're doing it then letting it hang there in time, almost like it's forming itself. Like a potter's wheel, a vase of clay, turning, and you just touch it, nudge it, shape it with your hands, but really it forms itself." I realised I was standing up, pacing, I had walked to the top of the room where the gap in the tables formed a natural stage. Everyone was watching me. "It's an epiphany. You'll get it when you get it."

"And you'll show us how, Jo, is that right?"

"Yes!" I looked from face to face. Dad, Louise, Jason, Josie; Peter had joined us after nodding in approval at my paint job that afternoon, and his wife, Ria, and their two daughters were here, too. Katrina with her wool, and her husband. Only Grandad wasn't laughing. He came up to me, looked kindly into my face and took my hand.

"I think you better sit down, Jo. You're over-excited."

I wanted to scream, and I felt the irony in that, too. But I had experienced something new, and I wanted to share it.

"But Grandad, I want everyone to understand."

"You can show us, Jo. Tomorrow. It's not doing any good talking about it now." I saw him frown around the room at the remaining smiles. "Leave her alone." It was unusual for him to get upset, and they all reined themselves in.

"It's all right, Grandad. Really it is."

He harrumphed, then subsided. The room went quiet. It was Ria who spoke next. "Did you all hear? Barry's closed up shop. They're leaving."

I turned to her, feeling my eyes and mouth sag. Barry ran the delicatessen, supplying all the interesting food locally, retailing the only organic vegetables in town. Lots of the growers relied on him. There was nothing to say. I sat still. Nothing to say, but maybe something to do. I stood up. "I'm going to see him. Maybe they'll come."

Their house was only three blocks away. In five minutes I was standing outside. What would I say? I had no idea, but I knocked anyway. Barry answered, his face sad.

"Hey Barry. I heard the news."

He nodded.

"Some of us are eating at Louise's tonight. We'd love it if you'd come."

"I don't know, Jo. We're not really in the mood for company."

"When are you leaving?"

"Not sure. End of the week, maybe."

I sniffed the air. No smell of cooking. "Dad's done a venison stew. It's good. Please."

He shrugged, turned in the doorway. "Helen! Jo's inviting us for tea."

His wife came to the end of the hall, bread knife in hand. "We were just going to have sandwiches."

"Well, bring the bread." I could see she was having difficulty with the decision. "Go on. Come." I took a step down the hall, my hand out as if to lead her. "Come."

17

Grandad sat on my bed, a tray in his hands holding toast and coffee. "It's good that you slept in, Jo. You've been working too hard."

"What time is it?"

"Eight thirty."

I rubbed at my face. "Shouldn't you be at work?"

"It's Saturday."

Saturday. Something clanged inside me. A disappointment. What was it? Ah! No guests for Louise's. I'd said Friday, and no-one showed up. I felt my bottom lip slide forwards. Plenty of time, I told myself, but really, I had expected a miracle. We needed some miracles.

"Have a piece of toast. I got that honey you like."

"Thanks."

We sat in silence while I chewed, but there was an edge to it, not like the simple companionship we usually shared. "Was there something else you wanted to say?"

"I'm worried about you, Jo. You're excited but you're not happy."

"Don't worry about me. Really. I've got a lot on my mind, but I can handle it."

"I wanted to help, but I never know what to say."

"Really . . ."

"So I called Malcolm. He said he'd talk to you."

"Grandad, I don't need . . ."

"You better get up now. He's coming at nine. He'll know what to do."

He nodded, task accomplished. I leaned back on the headboard. I did not want this. Malcolm was the minister of the local Presbyterian church. He ran the youth group I went to before I left for university. He knew me when I was young and lively and out of control. He was there when I went through my experimental swearing phase. He was there when I grew into my new body and didn't know how to move, awkward and embarrassed. "He thinks I'm still a kid!" I wailed.

Grandad looked worried. "Get dressed now. He'll be here. I'll take Dad out of the way so you can talk."

There was another complication. Dad and Malcolm had been at loggerheads since Malcolm cut down the big elm tree in front of the parsonage. He said it was blocking the light. Dad told him he was a butcher, nothing better than a soulless murderer. You can guess how that went down.

"Foreign upstart," I heard Dad muttering as Grandad ushered him out the door.

I threw Malcolm a rueful look, acknowledging the impossibility of an apology. "Please, have a seat. Cup of tea?"

"Thank you."

"Did Grandad say why he'd asked you to come?" I called as I filled the kettle. I switched it on then came back to the doorway to hear his answer.

"I gather he's worried about you. His reasons were less than clear. But I've heard bits and pieces around town. Why don't you tell me what you're up to?"

I searched his face for any trace of condescension. There was none. I trailed back into the room, draped myself over the arm of the sofa and began to talk. At first it tumbled out, randomly ordered. Then I found myself spilling out all my disappointment, all my discouragement that the people who had been so strong, so impermeable when I was a child, now showed so much weakness. "I understand. They're finding it hard to adapt. But they used to be the grown-ups. They were the ones who looked after me." I flicked a look up into his eyes, defensive. "Not that I need it now. I'm fine. I can look after myself. That's not the problem. The problem is whether I have the strength to look after all of them."

I waited for him to speak, but he said nothing. After five seconds of silence I was off again, into new territory, into the hugeness of the task ahead, into the overwhelm of all I had to do. The vision I had was enormous, way too big for one person. I found myself crying. "I told them I could do it. But I can't. I can't." Instinct told me to run for the door and keep running, but I didn't have the strength. I put my arm onto the back of the sofa, put my head down onto it and continued to cry. Malcolm stayed quiet, emanating waves of peace. Instinctively I felt for any sign of smugness, anything to divert attention from myself, make him the weak one. But there was none. He was just there, with me, ready to listen again when I was ready to talk.

"You're not saying anything."

"What would you like me to say?"

"That I don't have to do it. That it's crazy. That I'm too young, there's no way. Be the voice of wisdom. I'm not up to this."

" 'Let this cup pass away from me . . .' "

"What?"

"The words of Jesus, before the crucifixion. Do you know what came after?"

"No."

" 'Thy will be done.' He knew that he was the only one who could do it. And he was ready. Ready to trust that when the time came, he would do what he had to do. And you? What do you know?"

"I know I can do this. And I know that I have to. And I'm scared. I have no idea what I'm doing, where to start."

"That's a bit of a contradiction. You sound confused."

"I am confused!" I was shouting, and I hated losing it this way, in the presence of this too-calm man. His next words surprised me.

"Tell me about the confusion. What's it like?"

"About the confusion? . . . It's confusion. Isn't that clear enough?" He hadn't responded to my tears and he didn't respond to my anger. He just waited. I thought. "It's like darkness. Chaotic darkness. Like waking up in the middle of the night into a storm, pitch black, and objects hurtling around me. Smoke and wind and debris. It's all I can do to protect myself. I can't make sense of anything. And I don't know what will happen next."

"What would help?"

"It would help if I could see. If I had any clarity."

" 'Let there be light.' What else?"

"Wait a minute. What did you say?"

"I was quoting from the creation. It seemed appropriate. Your description reminded me of the time before the creation, when all was darkness and chaos. 'And God said, "Let there be light", and there was light.' You just have to ask for it. Ask for the help you need. What else?"

But I was silent, revolving this idea in my mind. The facts before me where overwhelming. Friends and family in need. Everything sinking fast. "I don't know what to do. When it seems I'm finally getting somewhere constructive there's another emergency, another sinking ship. I have to take out the lifeboat, perform mouth-to-mouth again. And in the meantime, there's no progress. I'm torn between first aid and a long-term strategy. My attention is split and I've fallen into the gap." I sat up straight. That was it. I was working towards a plan, and I kept getting distracted. "I need help. Someone to help me see clearly."

"Someone to talk to?"

"Yeah – but someone who gets it."

"Then ask."

"But where? Where would I find it? Who do I ask?"

Malcolm held his hands out. "What about me?"

I looked at him, dubious. "But you don't think I can really do it."

His brow and lips moved together, perplexed. "Why do you say that? Of course I do."

"But I'm . . ." I was going to describe myself as I knew he saw me. But it appeared I was wrong.

"Look, we get training. Counselling. Recently it's more flexible, constructive. Not about charity for the weak, although that's part of the job when it's needed. I prefer empowering others. Lifting them up and helping them see what they can be. And you already know what you can be, what you are. You just need a sounding board, to get things clear."

"And you'd do that?" It was like a curtain pulling back, the stage opening before me.

"It would be an honour." He grinned then. I realised something was different about him. The beard was gone. That clinched it. With the beard I wouldn't have been sure, but now this was a man I could talk to.

I smiled, gave a small laugh. "Okay. That'd be great. Thanks."

18

I went back to sleep after Malcolm had gone. The last night hadn't been long enough. An hour later I woke feeling clear and refreshed for the first time in weeks. I still didn't have a plan but I had a plan for how to make a plan, and that made me feel better. A miracle. Malcolm was doing his job!

I reached out of bed to get my notebook. Ideas were bursting in my head like popcorn: just as fast and just as random. If I wrote them down I might be able to get them in some sort of order.

There were two sorts of thoughts going on. The fire-fighting, first aid sort of activity I'd been doing since I realised what was going on: getting Josie out of bed, closing Louise's café, saving her house – and feeding them all, let's not forget that. And now I needed to persuade Barry and Helen to stay, to wait it out, to trust that once things got back on track, they'd have a thriving business again; the organic produce they brought together would be the cornerstone of our new town.

Then there were the positive future actions, as yet largely untouched, but sorting out Louise's house was a start, letting the tourist information office know about it. These were where my energy needed to go long term. Charity was a strictly temporary measure. As the old parable goes, I needed to teach these people how to fish; and while I was about it, it wouldn't hurt to set up a metaphorical fish farm to make it easier.

The Slow Town – a magnet for those tourists who might stay a while rather than just passing through – what did that consist of? All the usual stuff: cafés and banks and petrol station, maybe with a Slow slant, but basically as described elsewhere; and then the Slow amenities: Slow Food restaurants, Slow tourism, guided walks, horse trekking, craft workshops. I made a list of everything someone could do if they weren't in a hurry and was amazed at how many activities didn't make sense in a convenience paradigm, but looked appealing on the page in front of me.

I never understood knitting, but if you looked at it as something you did while you were deep in contemplation, or sitting talking to friends, it had a totally different aspect.

Cooking Slow didn't work if you were hungry right now and you hadn't planned it, but really, how much of a surprise was it that we needed dinner each night, breakfast each morning, lunch in the middle of the day?

I loved clothes, but I'd got used to throwing on whatever came first to hand in the morning, as I rushed from my room into my packed day. What if I took my time, enjoyed the moment, and then subsequently every moment of the day that little bit more, knowing that how I looked reflected something more of me? I really hated the same old jeans and sweatshirt – well, maybe not the jeans; perhaps there could be a gorgeous, sequinned top, or some handmade colour to go with them.

Images flashed in front of my eyes like a lightning storm, released from some long-locked corner of my creative mind and falling over themselves for instant expression and notice.

I put my pen in my mouth, an unexpected pause; I felt an almost audible click. Starting now, I would make some sacred spaces in my day. Choosing my clothes in the morning; planning the meals for the day and week, even if that just meant finding Dad and his Slow stew; taking five minutes to talk to Grandad, whenever it happened that I saw him for the first time on any given day. I knew he'd love that. He'd probably even notice. A smile opened my face up and it felt like sunshine. I'd call my friends, too, not just text to touch base. Maybe I'd even invite them to come and stay.

I looked down at my list once more. Okay. How much of this could I do myself, what could I find resources for inside the town, and where was I going to need to go outside, find investors, other people to make it work? I made marks on the paper, rewrote it into three lists, then numbered those in order time-wise. I would take action, it would be logical, and Slow would be created double quick.

Unusually aware, I felt a frown pass over my forehead. There was something else, something I had to do first, something I didn't want to think about. What was it?

Ahh, that! I had to call a meeting. I had to talk to the town. I felt a sinking dread and closed my eyes. Not today. Not today.

"Dad, how would I go about setting up a Slow Food restaurant? Who would I ask?"

"Why do you need one?" He was cutting vegetables and didn't look up.

I rolled my eyes. "That's the whole point, Dad. Haven't you been listening? Folkstown is going to be a Slow Town."

"But we already have a restaurant."

"What do you mean?"

"At Louise's."

"But, Dad, that's just a soup kitchen, charity, for people who can't afford to feed themselves."

It's not often I've seen him really angry. He seemed to grow six inches. "Are you telling me my food's not good enough for people who can afford to pay?"

"That's not what I mean! But it is what it is. A temporary measure. Till people get back on their feet again."

His glaring eyes continued to burn into my face.

"Come on, Dad! You knew that! It's just fact."

We continued to stare at each other for perhaps a minute longer. It felt like a very long time.

Finally he slapped down the knife he was holding into the middle of the pile of carrot slices and stormed out. Who'd have thought he'd be so touchy? Really, what did he think? But he was Dad, he'd come round. There was no-one else I could ask about this. I'd wait.

Two hours later he came home, picked up ingredients and utensils without speaking and was heading for the door again.

"Wait! Dad! Really. I need your help."

He sniffed. "I'm late already. I have to get this on. If you want to talk to me, come down to the restaurant." There was a slow sneer in this last word that I ignored. It wasn't going to be as easy to talk there, with whoever else happened to be around, but I had no choice. I went to get a jacket - a cool breeze was blowing - and as I came out I saw his car disappearing down the road. I pulled the door behind me with a bang and followed on foot.

The bell rang, announcing my entrance. Louise was wiping down tables. I could hear Dad chopping in the back, louder and faster than usual.

"He's still mad, then?"

"I've never seen him like it. What did you do?"

"Everyone's so quick to blame me! Nothing! He's so stubborn."

Her eyebrow tilted upwards and she turned to the next table. I took a deep breath and entered the kitchen, pausing with my mouth open, not knowing what to say. Dad had his back to me. Still, he must have known I was there, he was the first to speak.

"You think someone's a better person just because they have more money."

"They have higher expectations."

"You think I'm a worse person than I was when I had more money."

"No, Dad . . ."

"Or Louise?"

Her voice rang through from the other room. "You leave me out of this!"

"If people are paying more, they expect something more."

"So you're saying my food's not up there with the best of the best."

"You know it's great, Dad, it's actually great, but people need choice."

"Why? Why do they?"

How was I going to fight this one? "It's just the way it is, Dad. People want to have choice."

"Why? 'It's just the way it is'! Since when do you mindlessly go along with the status quo? The status quo would have the town go down. What we

95

have here is enough." He had turned to me now. His bottom lip was out like a grumpy little school boy.

I gave up on this point, moving on to the next. "Well, how do we run it, Dad? How do we make it pay at the same time as feeding the people who need it?"

"Easy. There must be a hundred ways."

"What?" I tried, unsuccessfully, to stop myself shouting. "What are they?"

"You are so stuck! Your mind is so stuck in the way things usually work. Get your head out of the box and think. A new perspective. A new way. You're the one with all the big ideas! Don't call it a restaurant if that makes you think too narrow. Look bigger. Think about what you actually want it to do."

I stared at him. It was like the whole world shifted, each molecule separately, like one of those kids' jigsaws on cubes, with a different picture on each face. The problem transformed into something totally new.

"Dad . . ."

"I'm actually busy here, Doll, in case you hadn't noticed. You get out and let me focus on producing mediocrity for the masses. Answer your own questions." His face softened. "You already know everything you need to know."

He walked across the room with a tea towel held out and herded me from the room. I felt Louise's eyes on me as I stepped through the outside door and heard her voice filter out as it swung shut behind me. "You're too hard on her."

And Dad's reply. "I know."

19

A Slow Town needs to provide Slow Food. That's a given. But beyond that? How far do we need to conform?

The standard restaurant format, separate individuals and groups coming in to sit at separate tables, choose from a menu, be served, it was fine as far as it went, but it wasn't essential. What were the alternatives? Something like we were doing already, with people interacting, telling stories, doing crafts. There must be a million possibilities once we got outside the standard description. So what did we need?

We needed it to pay its own way. Eventually to make money.

We needed to feed the people of the town who for whatever reason wanted it, and probably at low prices for at least some of the people some of the time. That reminded me of a restaurant I'd heard of, where people paid what they could afford, no judgement, put money in envelopes, and if they had nothing, helped out in the kitchen. I filed the thought.

What else?

A positive experience, and that was a flexible idea. Did it have to be the same as anywhere else? No. I guess that was Dad's point.

It had to provide excellent food.

And excellent ambience.

If there were only one option in town it had to cater to various dietary requirements: ideological, religious and sensitivities/allergies.

It had to manage a wide range of personalities and demographics, including the elderly and children and we had to consider facilities for disabilities. We wanted everyone to feel welcome, included.

It would be great if it were something unique, so we needed to set people up beforehand so they were prepared for something different.

Eventually, if all went well, we would need a bigger venue.

And then, it needed to be flexible enough that if someone came along and wanted to start something else, whatever that was, that would be fine.

My pen paused over the paper. There was more, I knew there was. I wasn't thinking wide enough. Give it time. Allow it to soak overnight. And ask some other people. Stop trying to do everything myself.

"Dad? Can I come in?"

"Sure, Hon. Come here." He held out his arm and I let him pull me to his side.

"I'm sorry."

"Me, too."

"I think your food is fabulous."

"I know." He handed me a plate. "Want some?"

"Yeah, please." He lifted the cooker lid and filled the plate with rich, brown stew, shining. I grabbed a piece of Louise's bread and kissed him before heading out to sit with Grandad. Family. It's great always knowing that, no matter what happens, with family, everything will always be all right.

20

Louise was telling a story. I had arrived in the middle so I struggled for a minute to get the context. I heard my name, and realised what was happening: the tourist information office had called to book in her first guests. But I had forgotten to tell Louise I had talked to Kathy about the bed and breakfast. It had come totally out of the blue. Oops. I opened my mouth to say something – to apologise, or make an excuse for myself – but Grandad put a hand on my arm to stop me, and in that moment's hesitation I heard something else: not a judgement on my thoughtlessness or incompetence, but the rhythm of a well-told story. My interruption wasn't necessary. She wasn't asking for an apology. The story wasn't even aimed at me. I sat back, heard the payoff and laughed with everyone else. The sideways glances that came my way I could even interpret as indulgent.

I lifted my hands. "Mea culpa."

"No big deal," said Louise. "It'll be my first income for weeks. Two nights, 600 bucks. A godsend. But they're arriving at four tomorrow. Think you can get the painting done by then?"

"Sure. If I work all night."

"I'll help," Jason chipped in. "I should have been there today."

The conversation shifted. I realised I felt peaceful, when in the past, in any comparable situation, I would have felt criticised, defensive and guilty. When had that changed? I leaned over towards Grandad, touching my shoulder to his.

"How was your day?"

"Good." That was his stock answer, developed to satisfy this social convention. In fact he was so in the moment, he probably would have trouble recalling the individual events of the last twelve hours. I tried to think what would be a more interesting question. What would draw him out, let him reveal something of himself? Suddenly I wanted to hear his stories, his unique perspective, more urgently than ever before.

"What you been doing?"

"Oh, you know, work. And your dad brought home some wood, I made a little table."

"Oh, yeah? What kind?"

His eyebrows twitched. The question confused him. "Guess you better take a look if you want. It's just a table."

I wanted to know more. A coffee table, a dining table? The workshop wasn't big enough for that, probably, but I wanted a clearer picture. He felt my frustration and shifted uncomfortably. I hated making him feel like this. "I'd love to take a look. When I get home."

He nodded.

"What are you going to do with it?"

Another unanswerable question. Why did I keep imposing my own calculations and motivations on him? He had made a table because the wood was there and he wanted to make a table. No other agenda. Once again I saw confusion and hurt in his eyes.

"I dunno. Maybe give it away."

"I'm sorry, Grandad. You don't have to know. I would love to have a look at it. Was it fun making it?"

At last, his eyes lit up. "Yeah, I enjoy it. I like looking at the wood and seeing the shapes, and deciding how to put it together. I like the feel of the wood, and sanding it smooth." His breathing evened out and his shoulders relaxed; his eyes were focused in the distance, on something I couldn't see. "Just like your dad is when he cooks."

"Really?"

"Yeah. And Louise when she's telling a story. People doing what people are supposed to do. Each one different."

I thought for a moment. Tried to make a joke. "And what about me? What do I do that's like that?"

Again the crease in the forehead. "You like making plans. Big plans. That's what you like doing. But it's not the same."

"Why isn't it? Why?"

"Well because . . . it's not the same. You get excited. You start rushing about. But then you get . . . disappointed. You like the seeing, the planning, but not the doing."

"What? That's not fair! I always follow through! I always do what I say I'll do."

"Don't get angry at me, Jo, I'm sorry. I didn't mean it."

I didn't mean it. Another one of his stock responses. But this one to get him out of serious distress, only used in emergencies. I put my plate down, turned and pulled him into a full body hug. Out of the corner of my eye I saw Louise watching. The room went quiet. Now everyone was staring. Grandad clung to me. I gestured to Louise, who started telling a joke, drawing everyone's attention again. I breathed a silent 'Thank you' and pulled Grandad away from me.

"I'm never angry at you. Never. I love you to the bottom of my soul. I just want to understand. You're so wise. I just want to see what you see."

At the word 'wise' he shook his head. His face was still sombre.

"But I really want to know what you meant. I think it can help me. What do you mean I don't like the doing?" Still he hesitated, like a spooked cat. "Please?" Slowly I felt his forearms relaxing under my hands. "Please? How is it different from you and Dad and Louise?"

He cleared his throat, pulled one hand away from mine to scratch his neck. "Well . . ." he sniffed, deep in thought. "We're happy doing what we're doing. We might have an end point we're heading towards, but each step is . . . nice . . . in itself. We lose ourselves, forget everything, just in the doing. When I watch you it's like . . ."

"It's okay. Really. You can say it. I'm calm now."

"Yeah, you are. Okay. It's like you're racing. Like you think someone else will get there first, or like something bad might happen before you're finished."

I sat back, hearing his words echo.

"That makes me scared when the plans are really big. Like when you went away to university saying about finishing in three years. I thought, 'Now she won't be happy for three years.'" His eyes widened. "And then it was four. Four years. It's too long."

"Is it?" I asked, absentmindedly. I was still absorbing the 'something bad' happening. "Four years isn't so long."

"Not long if you're living each day. But if you're waiting for something to be finished, just waiting and rushing . . ." he gave a shudder, and, after a moment, I found my body shuddering too.

SLOW TIME

21

We finished painting, then Jason and I pulled the furniture back through from the other room, being careful not to bump the walls, which were touch dry but needed to cure a little longer. We'd put the curtains up at the last minute. We laughed as we arranged the sofas and cushions, the photographs on the round table by the wall, then looked around. It was pretty good. Next thing was to go back into the dining room and sort that out, move the furniture away from the walls where we had stacked it and make it all look great, too. It felt fresh and lively, bright with the new paint.

"Now just the pictures. Want to call your mum so we can decide where they should go?"

"Sure." He backed out of the room, eyes on me. This made me momentarily uncomfortable, but I forgot it as I flicked through the picture stack, mentally reviewing where they had each been before.

Louise appeared.

"Okay, what say we go to the front door and do a tour as if we were guests arriving?" We all used the back door of Louise's house, so this view was novel.

"Come on out," she called. "See it from the path first, the veranda."

"You need some cane furniture."

She nodded. "Yeah. There are a couple of chairs in the shed. I'll have a look, see if we can clean them up."

"Front door needs painting."

"The whole house does, but yeah, just doing the door would help."

"I'll get on it."

"I can do it," Jason interjected. "I'll get the paint today." When did he get so eager to help?

"What colour?" Louise asked me.

"Black?"

"Good plan."

"Glossy black enamel," I told him, "But on second thoughts, I'll get it. I want to tell Peter he'll get some of his money on Wednesday."

Louise's face became nervous. "Will he? We could really use it all for the loan."

"Just $100, Lou. He's been very generous. He should know we're serious about repaying him."

"Okay. Sure. I guess."

"Especially as we're asking for more paint today."

She held up her hands. "I get it. I said 'yes' already."

"Okay. So here we are, at the front door. What do we want where?"

Grandad's table was gorgeous, about the size and height of a bedside stand, but it would probably look better in a living room. It was irregular – as he said, he had seen the shape of the wood and worked with it to produce a unique and beautiful piece. The base was more symmetric, splayed at the bottom like the spreading roots of a tree.

"It's wonderful. May I?" I reached out tentatively and lifted it off the ground. It was heavier than I expected. Using two hands I tilted it so I could look underneath. The wood was unfinished, and I could feel the powdery remains of sanding dust. The base fitted into a notch in the top and was anchored in place with a couple of cross pieces which were drilled through the wood. "This is great! I didn't know you could do this."

"It's obvious, really, you just look at it and it comes into focus." But I could see he was chuffed at my admiration. "The base unscrews, too, so it's easy to move, if someone wanted it sent somewhere."

"You're thinking of selling it?"

"Maybe. I seen other tables in the furniture shop. Not as good as this. They charge an arm and a leg. And your dad gets plenty of wood when people don't want it. Just used for firewood otherwise. I can make more. I like it, and my job's not going to last forever."

"They wouldn't let you go."

"Calm down, Jo. It's okay. They will if they have to, and it's okay."

"But . . ." I felt tears in my eyes. He put his arm around me.

"It's okay. Really. It's only change. And now I've found something new to do."

"Well, Grandad, I'll sell them for you. I promise."

"Calm down, Jo. Just let it take its time. It's much easier if things take their time."

I stared out the window, deep in thought. My hands had given up hovering over the keyboard and had come to rest under my chin. Sunlight sparked off Grandad's birdbath and I had been playing with it, absentmindedly, for a very long time, closing one eye and then the other, shifting my head an atom's width this way and that, delighting in the fractures caused when a bird stopped to wash, and losing myself anew in the flicking of the beads of liquid on its head, its back, the drops of water flying as it shook its wings.

I was supposed to be writing up my notes about our starting point: the financial situation of the businesses I had studied, the full list of the existing businesses and the ones that had already closed down. The final profile of the town would be different, if all went to plan, the cross-section of services altered from how I had known it all my life. I needed to read the Slow Charter thoroughly, to make sure we were heading right for that, but it was dull, the language verbose. It left me cold. I just wanted to feel my way there, to follow this seam of Slow, let my intuition guide me, tell me what a Slow Town needed.

Undisciplined.

I know.

A movement caught my attention and I saw Jason walking up the path, a grin on his face. I waved.

"How were the guests?"

"Cool. It's weird having strangers in the house, but Mum's over the moon about getting paid. We got another booking for the day after tomorrow."

"Fantastic! For how long?"

"Just a night. But still."

"Yeah."

His eyes fell, his feet started shuffling. "Hey, you want to go out? Celebrate? I'll shout you a coffee?"

"And where are we going to go? Minnie's?" He knew I wasn't serious. Louise and Minnie had been rivals forever. No-one knew how Minnie was hanging on. She had a few customers, but surely not enough to keep her going. She was one of the ones who had declined to talk to me. Old bad blood. Mum hadn't liked her much, either. Minnie used to teach at the school and Mum and Louise had been tearaways, challenging and disrespectful.

"We'll get a takeaway coffee from the dairy."

"And drink it on the street. Cool." Despite my sarcasm I stood up, pressed Control S to save my work and closed the lid of the laptop. I needed a break, and it was always relaxing being in Jason's company. Or at least it had been. I realised, as we walked, that there was something unsaid in the air.

"Come on. Out with it. What's on your mind?"

He looked up, guiltily, but refused to answer, making a couple of clumsy efforts to change the subject. Finally I let it go. He'd tell me in his own time.

I pointed at the dowdy building we were passing. "It's about time the town had somewhere decent to stay. Somewhere better than the Downtown Motels."

"Yeah, but can you believe people will pay $300 a night? It's outrageous."

"Keep your voice down."

"Sorry." He looked around furtively. "No-one heard," he whispered.

I laughed. "It's okay," I whispered back, exaggerated, loud. "You need to get out more. People pay thousands to stay at some of the top lodges.

We're not in that league, but $300's not that much. The suite'll be $400, maybe more, later."

"Well, anyway, it's huge what you've done. And I wanted to say 'thank you' – you know, properly."

"What do you mean, 'properly'?" I was tempted to laugh, he sounded so serious. He stopped and faced me, taking my hands. I looked over my shoulder. "We not getting that coffee?" He said nothing, so I turned back towards him. The look on his face was odd, and I tilted my head in a question. I didn't realise what was coming until too late, until he had leaned in towards me, a fast, nervous movement, and collided his lips with my own. "Jason!" For a moment my vision was blank, and when it cleared he was looking away. "What was that?"

"Nothing." A low mumble.

"No, not nothing. What were you doing?"

"Kissing you."

"Why?" Okay, it was a stupid question.

"Why not?"

"Because you're eighteen and I'm twenty-two. For goodness sake." I know, I know. Insensitive. I couldn't help it. I continued walking. He was silent at my side, then before we got to town, at the corner of his street, he turned and ran. God. I'm an idiot. What had I done?

22

"Damn!" I stood still on the street feeling foolish. Where was I going to go now? Finally my footsteps lead me forward on auto-pilot and I found myself standing outside the dairy without the will to go in. Malcolm's church was across the road. Maybe I'd find refuge there.

I sat in one of the back pews looking forward towards the altar and the stained glass windows. The patina of years of worship filled the air, calming, bringing perspective. Damn Jason! As if I didn't have enough to worry about; but sitting there, I knew my worries were temporary – things would work out. Maybe I should come here more often. My lips turned gently upwards. My family didn't exactly have a history of conformist church-going. Weddings, funerals, christenings, that was it. But just those events had brought me here many, many times. And the Christmas services. I loved carols. Not many weeks now till Christmas rolled around again.

The door opened behind me.

"I thought you were going to call me. Set up a coaching session."

"I was. I am. A lot has been happening."

"And how are you?"

"I'm fine."

Malcolm peered into my face. "No, you're not. Do you want to do that session now?"

"You've got time?"

"I have."

"Well, okay." I didn't feel prepared. But maybe I never would.

"Come next door. The study's quiet."

I followed him meekly out.

The winged armchair was a little daunting at first, but then I got to like the way it surrounded and protected me. Malcolm sat in a similar chair, the pair of them arranged around the fireplace, set at this time of year with ornamental pinecones and dried flowers.

"Tell me what's been happening."

"You know about Louise's house."

"Yes."

"And we're playing with the idea of making the Slow Food café a paying business, maybe letting people choose what to pay."

"How would that work?"

"I'm still figuring out the details."

"Would you like to do that now?"

"Maybe once I've got everything else clear."

"What else is there?"

The image of Jason fleeing flickered through my mind. I shuddered. I'd think about that later. I was worried about him, but it was a distraction. Focus. "I'm thinking longer term, about accommodation in the town. We need more than just Louise's – the motel isn't really up to much."

"Fred wouldn't be pleased to hear you say that."

"That doesn't make it untrue."

Malcolm inclined his head.

"The thing is, it all comes down to money. We're still doing first aid, free food, keeping people afloat. How are we going to get more accommodation built – good quality accommodation – with the funds we have access to? It keeps coming back to that. And yet, I know there must be a way. Then I think of getting investment, but something tells me that's not it, that for now we need the extra wealth coming in to go to the families who already live here. It's a catch 22. We need money to make money. And a big build like that – I'm not qualified to project-manage it, and no-one else is, either."

"You say a big build. Does it have to be?"

"What do you mean?"

"Could you do it in smaller bites? One unit at a time. Expand gradually."

I stared at him. He was right. I had been thinking along the lines of a big new hotel, or a lodge, something like that. But maybe we could do it in self-contained units and start small. But where? Then it hit me. Everywhere. Anyone who wanted one could have one on their property. Small, self-contained units, easy to build, each one providing income for the family who housed it, each one with its own family flavour; managed centrally, booked centrally, but spreading the wealth through as much of the town as wanted a part of it. I let the idea sit for a moment. Malcolm waited. Finally I nodded. "Great idea."

I sat back in my chair, a vision taking form. I'd seen some little eco-cabins in a magazine, self-contained, environmentally friendly and very cute.

"I'd been thinking we needed a big piece of land, which would mean funding to buy it. But what if we spread them around the town? The idea, the whole idea, is about the town anyway." Most of us had big front lawns we did almost nothing with. There were some nice gardens, but these eco-cabins would blend well even there. "The cabins could even become a sort of signature for the town." My eyes blurred off into the distance. Remotely I noted Malcolm's patience. I was only speaking a very sketchy amount out loud.

This was do-able, whereas what I'd considered before was not.

"It comes back again to that meeting . . ."

"What meeting?"

"The one where I talk to the town, fire them up, sell them my vision." I sighed, and my shoulders slumped.

"And when do you plan to do that?"

"That's just it. I can't. I can't see past it."

"Why? What have you to fear?"

I looked at him as if he was mad. "What have I to fear?" His question pulled in such a traumatic, telescoping reality that I started to shake. "What about the possibility of totally messing up? Of giving them hope and then leaving them deeper in the shit than before? What if they invest time and money and energy and it doesn't work out? What if I fail them?" Image after image flooded through my mind: For Sale signs, funerals, goodbyes of one sort of another; the shop fronts dark. And one after another, endless glassy stares of accusation: Dad, Grandad, Louise, Josie, Jason . . . Peter . . . Malcolm. And at the back of it, representing the triumph of the devil, Minnie, her black teeth-gaps cackling like the mouth of Hell.

"Private failure would be bad enough, but if I failed my family, my friends, I think I would die."

I leaned my head on the arm of the chair and began to cry again, noisily, embarrassing myself; but it was also a blessed relief.

Malcolm waited, let me cry myself out. Finally I reached out to his desk and pulled a tissue from the box there.

"All right. Done with the self pity?"

I tried to be offended but only managed a pale laugh. "I guess so."

"And given those are the options: success or failure; giving them a new life or giving them false hope, only to be dashed, are you going to stop? Are you going to give up, go away, live your own life leaving those you love behind you? Or are you going to take your courage in your hands and get on with it?"

"I don't know!" I put my arms over my head and shook it back and forth.

His voice became gentle. "You can walk away, you know. No-one would blame you. You have a choice." I peered up at him. "You have a free choice. Yes or no."

I tried to let his words sink in. My chest was constricted. I didn't have a sense of choice there. There was a strait-jacket which tied me every way. "You don't understand. I have to do this. I can't fail. And I know I might."

"Stop. Stop right there. If you go into it with that belief, you're stuck, you're trapped, and your creativity will lose its power. Don't you sense that already? I've heard more 'can't' from you today than in your whole life before. If there's a trap, only you can release it. You need to acknowledge your right to choose."

"But I have to . . ."

He held up a finger. "No. Open your eyes. See a bigger picture. Take a step back, out of today's limited circumstances. No-one's going to die if you don't do this."

"Can you be sure?"

"Well if you're going to play that game, can you be sure no-one will die if you do do it, and do it perfectly?"

I blew out my breath. "Shut up."

"Manners."

I closed my eyes tight.

"Come on, Jo. See the choice. See your freedom. Without that freedom you're sure to fail, one way or another. Come on!"

"Don't rush me!"

"All right." He fell silent, and I allowed the room to slip away. I took a visual journey, up and out, looking over the town, sliding back and forward in time. I took refuge for a moment in earlier times, before this hardship, and then before my mother's death, when life was safe and simple. I slid forward, seeing the future, seeing it many ways: happy, sad, lonely, thriving. I saw the town diminished and felt a sadness that was personal, but not life-threatening. Then I saw it as my vision had begun to show me, alive, relaxed, full of love. Malcolm was right, I had a choice, and things would be okay either way.

He must have seen the change in my face. I was peaceful, myself again.

"So are you going to do it? Are you going to try?" he whispered.

"Yes." My voice croaked and I cleared it. "Yes," I said more strongly. "Yes, I am."

23

I stood in the church watching friends and family file in. My stomach was in knots and my hands were alternately squeezing each other white. I wanted to bolt and run. I knew I had to do this. I knew it. But it was hard.

In two days' time, on Christmas Eve, they'd all be back here again. I had wanted to leave this till the New Year, till after the holidays. Any excuse to delay.

"No, Jo, let's give them some Christmas hope."

There were lots of smiles, greetings, chatter. It was past seven, but the usual stragglers would be a few minutes yet, and full of excuses. Like you could get caught in traffic in Folkstown.

Malcolm came in with the mayor, James Smith, father of the notorious Bryan. I shook his hand. "Malcolm's told you what I'm thinking about?"

"Yes."

"And you're okay with it? I should have come to talk to you before, it's just it's all been . . ."

"It's okay, Jo. I think it's a great idea."

My shoulders relaxed. "Thanks. Thanks." I nodded, put my hand on his arm, then my attention was called in another direction, another group to greet: Barry and Helen, who, in response to my impassioned begging, had agreed to hang on in their organic delicatessen and vegetable store a little longer. I shook their hands, smiling, then walked to the front of the church and looked around.

Malcolm caught my eye and made a calming gesture, lowering his hand flat towards the floor. I wanted to go to the bathroom but it was too far away, on the other side of the car park, off the church hall.

It's only nerves. You'll be fine when you get going, I told myself. Yeah, right.

The church bell rang and the chatter died down. The crowd turned expectantly towards me. Malcolm had offered to do an introduction, but I wanted this to be as informal as possible.

"Hey there, everyone." I gave a nerdish wave.

"Hey, Jo."

I grinned back. "Most of us know why we are here, what this is about, but I'll just fill in from the beginning so we know we're on the same page.

"Most of us know that the increase of in-car navigation systems in hire cars has meant that tourists are changing their route. Not so many of them are passing through the town."

There were nods and murmurs of agreement.

"When I came back for the summer I was upset to see the changes – it's subtle, but it had already made a big difference to some of the businesses." More nods. "While some of you are still doing fine, we're all tied together. What's bad for some is usually bad for all, in the long run. Do we all agree?" This time I waited for a response. I wanted everyone involved in the discussion, even though I would do most of the talking at the start. "Well, do we? Dad, Peter, Josie, Malcolm?" One by one the people I called on assented. A couple of others looked sceptical. I noted who they were; I'd get to them later. "Okay. So that seemed scary for a while, until I figured something out . . ." I waited till the pause became awkward.

"What? What did you figure out?" It was Peter. I could always count on him.

Now I grinned. Against all expectation, I was starting to have fun. "I figured out that if what's bad for some is bad for all, then what's good for some is also good for all."

"Well, so? What's been happening that's good?"

I shrugged. "Anybody think of anything?"

"You closed down my café," Louise shouted. There was a scattering of laughter.

"But then she did up the house." I turned towards where Jason was leaning against the side wall. I hadn't seen him come in. I tilted my head, gave him an apologetic smile.

"And we've got Dad's Slow Food restaurant started, that's got to be good."

"Is that a restaurant? I thought it was a charity house."

"Well, you can just shut up, Peter Baggins. I don't hear you complaining when you come back for third helpings." I wasn't sure if Dad's indignation was real or for show. I jumped in before an argument could take root.

"The restaurant is one of the best things, not just for what it gives us now, but for the direction it suggests." I stepped forward and intensified my expression as I looked deliberately from face to face. "I asked myself what had caused the change, and what we could do to reverse it, alter its course.

And I realised, with Grandad's help, that what had caused the change was the worldwide epidemic of hurry. The thoughtless drive for efficiency. It would take three minutes longer to drive through Folkstown. One kilometre more. And these people are on holiday. Why would three minutes, one kilometre, make a difference when they have flown thousands of miles to be on holiday in the most beautiful place on Earth? It doesn't make sense."

I looked around. People were nodding, foreheads creased in thought. "And then I thought, what's the antidote to rush? And there it was in front of me, in the thoughtful dinner my Dad served up every night. Slow. Going Slow. Slow Food. Slow Time . . . Did you know this is a worldwide movement? I looked it up on the Internet, and there's this whole community of people around the world searching for Slow. How to live thoughtful lives. It started with Slow Food, and now there's Slow everything, even Slow Cities. A city can sign a charter for lots of things that improve the way of life, centre it on people again, instead of on efficiency. Space for pedestrians instead of just wider roads for faster cars. Encouragement of local food and crafts rather than mass-produced imports. I've got to tell you, it appealed to me at a deep level. I've been rushing, working my tail off for the last four years. I know you all work hard, too. What if we could slow down a little, enjoy life a lot? And the other thing about these Slow Cities, Slow Towns – they attract tourists, and not just people who pass through for lunch, people who are moving Slow, who come to stay, for days, for weeks. And I thought – yeah, that's what we need. That's what could make a big difference."

I looked around again. People were turning to each other, eyebrows raised. Then the questions started.

"How do we do it?"

"How long will it take?"

"How's that going to help me?"

I held up my hands. "You're right, it's not an instant fix. It's not going to make things better overnight. We'll all have to tighten our belts a bit, weather things for a while. There's work to do. But I think it makes sense in the long term. Who agrees?"

A few hands went up. I waited. Gradually around half the church had voted for us.

"I'm just not sure, Jo."

I looked at Helen. I knew it took a lot of courage for her to speak, for her and Barry to even be here, to change their minds after they had already made the sickening decision to go. I was going to have to take a stand now, make a promise. Part of me wanted to avoid it, leave the responsibility with the room. But that was cowardly.

"Do you trust me?"

Her eyes flicked sideways, head twitched in a momentary tilt. "I guess."

"I won't lie. There are no guarantees. But I'm sure this is the way to go. Our best shot. So are you with me?"

She stared into my eyes for a long moment. I saw all her pain and uncertainty. And I got it. I felt it, deep in my chest. Finally she nodded. "Okay."

There was a smattering of applause. "So tell us, Jo. What's first?"

"Well, we need a web-site. I'll talk to some of the kids from the high school. Jason, will you help?" He nodded, a half smile, ironic, playing on his lips. I could feel his pain, too. "And we need to see about how to apply for

Slow City status. There's some information about that in the Charter, but we need to do some more research. Any volunteers to take that on?"

James, our mayor, stepped forward. "I think that's my department." People looked around, heads nodded.

"Great, thank you." I smiled, a lush, grateful smile which brought a glow to his cheek and eye. He looked more like his son than I had realised.

"And then, we need some Slow accommodation . . . now, I've got an idea of how we can do that without it costing a fortune." I outlined my plan of a unit or two on every property that wanted one, with some quality control. Grandad would oversee it, with his eye for detail and sense of the wider view. I explained how Dad's restaurant would grow, too, and my idea for entertainment, for a unique experience, for a growing gathering of story-tellers. "It's new and it's evolving. I'm not sure exactly where it will take us." I shrugged again. "But I'm excited. I love having a direction, and hope. I'd love for us all to take it on together. Who's with me?"

And this time, four-fifths of them raised their hands, and each of them spilled me a smile.

24

The project seemed no less daunting, but now I had a team behind me, and everything was out in the open. There was no hiding now. Failure would be public failure, but it would also be shared failure, and surely that wasn't as bad. Anyway, I preferred to think it would be shared, public success. Yes. Stick to that. I might just have to be flexible on the timeframe, given the newness of everything.

I sent my supervisor a long-overdue update email, telling her what I was doing, describing last night's meeting. I got back an out-of-office reply saying she was away till the fifteenth of January. For a moment I was disgruntled. You'd have thought she'd tell me she was going away. "But you were supposed to contact her three weeks ago," my conscience whispered. "Okay. Okay."

So I was on my own academically for a bit longer. That was fine. Plenty to do in the meantime, and I was keeping my notes up-to-date, outlining the events and decisions of each day.

"Are you going to take a break soon, Jo? Your dad's got the tree up, and I've unpacked the decorations."

I looked up from my laptop, feeling my chest expand. Maybe I could take the pressure off for a little while, think about something else, something here and now and immediate.

"Yeah, I'm coming now." I closed down the lid of the computer and felt for a moment like a bird taking flight.

We sat on the floor in the middle of the tinsel and lights, untangling coloured glass baubles and a few home-made family ornaments. Dad came out of the kitchen with a plate of iced biscuits and I had a reverberating sense of déjà vu, the years echoing backwards to before the time of the widowers. Thank goodness for the sunshine streaming in; without it I would have broken down and cried. Grandad took a biscuit from the plate, a beaming smile on his face. "Amelia's favourite recipe." I wondered how he could remember without the overwhelming melancholy that took me. He turned to me with a mischievous grin. "You know, sometimes I'd get her to make these for me when it wasn't even Christmas. She was a good woman. So kind." Still his eyes were sparkling. I wiped away a tear. I sank my teeth into the still-warm sweetness and felt a little better.

Dad took one end of the string of lights from me and I fed it out to him as he wound it round and round the tree. I occupied myself with identifying the different colours of the lights, darkened in their off-state, trying to imagine them lit. I was absorbed in a sense of discontinuity, of the unreality of knowing something but not experiencing it in the moment. Like when it was winter I couldn't imagine summer; when it was night I couldn't imagine daylight. Not properly. And with my mother and grandmother gone, I couldn't quite recall the sense of them being there. It

124

made me fear for the other people I loved. If I lost them they would truly be gone.

Grandad reached out for my hand. His instinct was uncanny, unsettling for a moment. "We're here now. It's enough." I looked into his eyes and my momentary disquiet dissolved. His hand was warm and safe and real.

He pulled me up and passed me a length of tinsel. The gold and silver were the most lush, but I liked the personality of the red and green and blue. The three of us wound it into the branches, weaving in and out of each other's arms. Then one by one we placed the hanging ornaments, with our varying strategies of order combining into chaos. Finally Dad brought the ladder and I climbed up to put the angel with her feather wings onto the top.

I ran to pull the curtains, artificially darkening the room, then we waited with breath held while Grandad plugged in the lights, counted down from ten and flicked the switch. Magic. I was seven again, eight, nine, fifteen and twenty-one. The years of my life telescoped back towards me till I knew I was grown-up once more. I hugged both these beautiful men.

"It's lovely, isn't it?"

"It feels like Christmas really now."

The carol service passed, Christmas morning with our hand-made presents, Dad's Slow Cooked chicken which fed half the town. There was a buzz in the air at Louise's café. Everyone contributed their favourite dish to the lunch; the food was traditional, but the conversation was not. The talk was not of Christmas, and there was none of the usual postprandial torpor;

instead, starting here and there like it was accidental, the talk was of plans for the future.

A few of the men gathered around Grandad to talk about the eco-cabins we were planning to build. Josie pulled in a couple of her best mates and they were whispering together, glancing up every now and then. When I caught her eye she flashed me a smile. I hadn't seen her so enthusiastic, ever. I was curious, but I wasn't being invited over.

Only Jason sat aloof. I pulled a chair up to his. The silence between us was wretchedly awkward. "Jason . . ."

He turned his twisted face away. "Please don't say anything."

"I have to. We can't keep on like this, not talking. I miss you."

His eyes swivelled back to my face and I felt sick at their expression.

"What can I do? I want to fix this."

He shook his head, looked down at his hands. "You can't fix it. I don't know what happened, and I don't know what to do about it. I can't change the way I feel."

"Not even for me?" The joke was weak and fell flat. I felt helpless. Clichéd advice spun through my mind: get busy, distract yourself, time will change you. I had the sense to keep it in; it would have been stupidly cruel to say it.

"Did you ever feel like this?"

"I'm not sure. I don't really know what you're feeling."

"Did you ever love someone, and have them reject you?"

I recoiled from the word, but instinct told me not to deny it. Only he could say whether it was love or not. If he said it was, I had to respect it.

My eyes flicked around the room as if I would find an answer there. "No. I don't think I've ever been in love."

"You see! I knew it! You don't know yourself. And you don't know me."

"Maybe you're right. Maybe there's something wrong with me." My eyes came to rest on his face, which was disturbingly hopeful again.

He shook his head eagerly. "You just have to give yourself time. Like you said, You've got a lot on your mind. Maybe when things ease up a bit..."

My gut told me to contradict him, to put an end to his hope, here and now. But I felt too ignorant, too inexperienced. For all I knew, he might be right. I had no history to go by.

"My friend Caroline, she's been in love since I met her, with someone, then someone else, and now this steady guy. I asked her once how she did it."

"And what did she say?" His voice was too eager, too cheerful. Alarm bells rang in my head.

"She just stared at me, for the longest time, and then said, 'How do you not?' "

"And then what did you say?"

"Nothing. Just sat there feeling like an idiot. Like I do now." I excused myself, closing the door on Louise's primitive ladies' room, shutting myself away from the crowd. Eyes on my eyes in the mirror, I gave a split-second, mirthless laugh. And you thought you'd come so far.

SLOW TIME

25

Three days after Christmas, I got on the bus for Wanaka. I was looking forward to this break, a few days with Caroline, beautiful scenery, a great party, time to reflect. I watched out the window as the South Island rolled by: Tekapo, Pukaki, a glimpse of Aoraki. The long Twizel straight streamed by then we were into the magic of the Lindis Pass, summer-gold, empty, like a different world.

Caroline picked me up from the little town centre, near the lake, where the bus stopped.

I stared at the small, red car. "What is this?"

"I know, totally impractical! No, the boot's here, at the front. It's a Porsche Boxster. My mum's. She's always wanting me to go driving in it with her. We went to Hokitika for lunch the other day. We were in the car for about ten hours."

"It's gorgeous!"

Caro's eyes sparkled. "Yeah. I know." The smooth paint shone in the sunshine. I opened the passenger door and the seat welcomed me like a well-worn glove. "Let's go home. Everyone's waiting."

"Everyone?"

"Mum, Dad, Mikey . . ." My heart fell a little. I love Mikey, but I had thought I would have Caroline to myself. "And my Uncle Dan's here. He's interested in your Folkstown project."

I shrugged, paying more attention to the way the car moved, sinuous, like it was stuck to the road by some sort of suction, than to her words. We wound around a few corners, more of the lake coming into view, then up a short side road to where her family's home perched on a low hill overlooking the water. We approached from the back, a wide turning-circle in front of two large garages, the main door between opening onto steps down into the vast living floor.

We stepped down into the middle of a panorama; I held my breath so I wouldn't make a fool of myself. Then Caroline's mother appeared out of nowhere, sweeping me into a full body hug.

"How's the genius? First Class Honours! We always knew you were something special."

"Hey there, Mrs Matthews."

"Oh, God, Honey, that makes me feel so old. Call me Viv, or nothing." She turned to Caro. "Did you see your dad and Dan in town? They walked in to get some bread for dinner."

"No, but we were just in and out of the car park. I'll show Jo her room. Where's Mikey?"

Viv pointed towards the deck where I could see a pair of feet tapping on the end of a slatted wooden recliner. Caro grinned. "We'll see him later. Here, come downstairs. Your room has a great view."

As if they didn't all! Downstairs was like a hotel, with door after door opening off one side of a curving hallway, built around the side of the hill. High windows and low wall lights lit the space on the hill side.

Caro gestured to a door. "This is me . . . and Mikey." She glanced at me, and quickly away. "You're here." She opened the next door and we stepped into a small paradise, tasteful beige on beige on white with accents of black and the lake feeling like it was in the room with us.

"Wow!"

"I know. Cool, huh! Who'd have thought they could come up with something like this without me here to supervise."

I thought of our student flat in Christchurch, basic and small, and the way Caroline fitted in there as if she'd known no other life. And the way she accepted the mattress on my bedroom floor at home, cheerful and grateful. I turned and hugged her. "This is so gorgeous. I feel out of place."

"Don't be silly. Mum and Dad love having guests. And you know I'm ecstatic you're here."

"You've got Mikey."

She smiled, blissful, like a Botticelli angel. "I know. And now you've arrived there is nothing else to wish for. Come on. Come and say hi."

The outside door was wide open and I could see Caro's dad and someone else at the barbeque. Mikey was helping Viv load drinks onto a tray. He leaned over and kissed me on the cheek. Brotherly. That's how I felt about Mikey, like he was a little brother. Like Jason. I cringed momentarily, then distracted myself by wondering why I felt older. Mikey was the same age as us, finished his degree and working for an engineering firm in Christchurch. Caro doted on him, looked up to him, but from my perspective there was something missing. Just as well, I guess. It would be beyond awkward if I fancied him, too.

Viv handed me a drink. I wondered what was in it. Something alcoholic, with fruit exuberantly brimming from the top of the glass. "So what are you going to do now that your degree is finished?"

I looked for Caroline. I thought she said she had talked about what I was doing. "I've got a project going, at home. I'm hoping there's a Ph.D. in it, but really it's about building up the town."

Viv shook her head so that her curls bounced from side to side. "I don't know how you do it. But you were always the clever one. Caroline's like me. Simple. An artist."

I wasn't fooled. She was loving and kind and generous, but she wasn't stupid. I knew most of the financial success came from Viv's astute handling of the business side of the family firm. She liked to present this feminine image socially, but in the office she was a tiger, smart and fast and ruthless. I admired her. She had everything material just the way she wanted it, and then she had the knack of letting it all go and focusing on people, as if none of it mattered at all.

"Caroline's like me," she repeated, "but you're more like Dan. Have you met him? He's around somewhere."

I pointed out onto the deck.

"Ah, yes. Dan! Come and meet Jo."

Both men came inside. Caroline's father Russell is big and solid and kind, with soft, warm eyes. He pulled me into a bear hug, and when I surfaced, his arm still around me, I put my hand out towards the slimmer, younger man behind him.

"This is my brother," Viv said. I felt my eyelashes flutter downwards in a way they never had before, shying from the yellow-green eyes, the faint smile.

"Caroline's been talking about you non-stop." He shook the hand I offered. It was a moment after he let it go that it began its slow fall back to my side. My mouth swerved upwards into a half smile and back again, not quite making it. I couldn't think of an answer. "I'm interested in what you're doing. I've just finished a development along Lake Wakatipu, an eco-hotel. Maybe you'd like to see it?"

I glanced around again for Caroline. She was just stepping into the room. I gave her a begging, helpless look. She tilted her head at me, as if to ask what was wrong, and finally answered for me. "I thought we'd go up on New Year's Day, if you're keen. Queenstown's always quiet the morning after."

I nodded, dumbly.

"Tell me what you're doing. We're thinking of the Slow Food option for our restaurant. That part's not open yet. How does what you're doing work?" Dan backed away towards the sofa and sat down. Russell let me go and faded away. I hardly noticed. I lost track of Caro, too, as I sat down on the other end of the long sofa, body turned towards Dan, one leg tucked up under me. I swallowed, and finally found my voice.

"We're just starting, just experimenting. It's my dad, really. He's the enthusiast. The idea came from him."

"Well, but describe it for me. It can't work on the normal restaurant model."

My brain slowly clanked back to life as I searched for words. Something held me back from describing the need of the town, the benevolent aspect of serving food to those who might otherwise go hungry. I wanted to spin it as a lifestyle choice, with dignity, as it would be once everyone got back on their feet. I found it a transforming exercise, speaking from the vision, the future, rather than the present. In a feat of grammatical daring, I managed to paint from the intention, and make that clear without opening the question of how it contrasted with now. Dan was a good audience, and I found my thoughts coming into focus as they poured into his ear. He asked astute questions, and in thinking through the answers, my plans developed, I became more and more animated. This could become addictive.

At the start I had avoided his eyes, turning my gaze from spot to spot on the spotless ceiling so I could create the visions in my head. Further into the conversation I found my eyes on his face, on his lips as he spoke, finding something there that reflected me back to myself, but altered, improved.

"What about your development. How did it start?" And now I could really watch him, see his passion. It was like watching the sky on Guy Fawkes night.

"Dinner's up!" Viv called. We both started.

Dan's brow furrowed. "Why didn't you call me? I was going to help Russell with the barbeque."

Viv only laughed and inclined her head towards the door, and the outdoor table beyond. We stood. I smoothed down my clothes, wishing I had dressed with more care. I felt out of place in this rich and famous setting, especially next to this elegant, charming man.

26

Next morning Viv and Russell were pulling together the last details for the party in two days' time. Caroline and Dan were debating what we could do that would take us out of the way, and the next thing I knew, the exploration party had been brought forward from New Year: Caroline, Mikey, Dan and I would visit his development an hour and a half away on the other side of Queenstown, along the lake towards Glenorchy.

"Get your jacket, we're leaving in ten," Caro called. I felt my stomach contract.

"Don't your mum and dad want help with the party?"

"Nah, they're better arguing it out alone. It's really not that complicated, they just like to make a bit of a fuss. Lengthens out the fun. So come on, get moving."

I gathered my notebook and camera so I could hide some of my discomfort under the cover of research. I found myself standing next to the car with Dan, waiting for the others - it's an irritating habit of Caroline's, she hurries everyone else then takes an age to get ready herself.

"You sure you want to do this? This is supposed to be your holiday."

"It's cool. I want to show you anyway, get your input."

"I'm not sure what I'd be able to offer.'

"You're too modest. Caroline told me about your honours project, your business sense."

"Caroline's an artist. She's . . . I mean, she doesn't . . . she's biased."

"Has she really fooled you? She's got a great business head on her, good judgement. She just hides it well. And she speaks highly of you."

I dipped my head. "She's too kind."

"Well, anyway, I enjoyed our chat yesterday. I'm sure we'll have stuff to say once we get there."

Mikey ambled up, and after a few minutes Caroline followed.

"You want to drive or shall I?"

Caroline laughed. "My Toyota or your BMW? Let's see . . . I think yours."

Dan blipped the remote and opened the driver door. I went for the back seat, but Caro shook her head, hanging off Mikey's hand. "I'm sitting with my boy. You go in front."

We took the Cardrona road, following the smooth slopes up to the Cardrona Hotel and then into the more challenging winds of the range. I felt my chest expand as we rode through the constantly unfolding desert views. There was a lot of traffic, but something about the BMW's presence made them pull off the road in front of us, giving us a clear run through to the Queenstown highway.

The main feature of Dan's hotel was its relative invisibility. Faced with local stone and natural wood it all but disappeared into the hill. It was below the road, with trees growing close in. The build can't have been easy, keeping the vegetation healthy as well as managing the steeply sloping site.

From the main building we could see a number of separate units built close to the stony edge of the lake.

We walked into the reception area, clearly taking the receptionist off guard. She slid her magazine under the counter and stood up straight. Her eyes raked over Dan and her tongue came out, running over her lips. I was surprised by a sudden desire to attack her, the shock of the emotion luckily fixing me to the spot.

"Hey Katie. We're just going to take a look around. Which units are empty?"

She took her time lifting off keys on coloured rings and handing them to him. I saw her fingers casually brush his palm as he took them, her eyes lingering on his face. He didn't notice, just thanked her and turned away down the hall.

"Follow me." He pushed open double doors with a confident sweep and stepped back to hold one wide. Moving past him was like passing through an electric field. "The restaurant is here, and a dozen rooms. The rest of the accommodation is in the pods. I don't know what you were thinking of," he addressed me directly, "but we found double structures were the most cost-effective while still offering privacy and plenty of view from each one. I'll show you the plans later, but let's look around first." The restaurant was empty, a large space with natural slate floors on three levels, like banked theatre seating, and a whole wall of windows towards the lake. The view was a carbon copy of the one from reception, lake relatively narrow at this point, the opposite hill filling the visual field; with the stepped floor, however, there was an additional element of drama.

"We rushed to get the rooms open before Christmas, get some income streaming, but at the moment there's only a limited room service menu, no full-time chef and we're still waiting delivery of the tables and chairs. My fault. I wanted to see the room finished before I decided on material."

"What did you go for?" Caroline asked.

"Wood in the end. I thought maybe glass but the space needs warming."

She nodded. "Good call. And this is the kitchen?"

We peered in at sleek stainless steel in long runs of benches, large ovens, racks of hooks, echoing and empty.

"You had a chef design it?"

"The owner of Majesty in Queenstown, on a consulting basis. He'll help us get set up when we're ready to go, oversee the staff part-time." Dan turned from Caro to me. "I'd like to talk to your dad, though. Alistair's great, but he comes from the restaurant paradigm. I like the sound of bringing an element of home in, something maybe a little simpler than usual. I'm not sure what, exactly, but I have a sense of something I could learn."

I swallowed, then coughed. "I'm sure he'd be happy, any time."

"Maybe I'll come visit, once you're back."

I worked to keep my face passive. "Sure. Cool." Out of the corner of my eye I saw Caroline's eyes narrow and then her mouth stretch in a smile. I turned my back on her, running my hand over a bench, pretending I was interested in the texture. All I needed was for her to start teasing. I'd probably fall apart.

27

Next, Dan took us out to some of the units, following a curving path down towards the lake and branching off to each small building. From the rear they had the presence of Irish cairns, mounds of stone with only narrow slits disguising a pattern of windows that would let light into the interior but gave perfect privacy.

A keypad allowed entry, and there was a voice phone also. "Last thing you want is to get all the way down here and realise you've forgotten the code. We can remote release the lock, too. I like redundant systems so that no matter what goes wrong it all works." He pushed the door open and we entered a Tardis-like cavern, spacious and bright, again with floor to ceiling windows facing the lake. Out front was a deck angled off to the left, a trellis dividing it from next door. "At the back here are kitchen and bathroom. Sleeping above, living at the front. It's simple and functional."

"And beautiful," I whispered.

Caro sniggered behind me, but when I turned her face was straight. "You said you've got guests already?"

"A few. About a third full. It's good. It'll build up. My work's nearly done here. Just get the restaurant going, then I need to look for something new." Dan turned to me. "That's why you fascinate me." I'm sure I blushed to the ends of my fingers. "What you were saying about Slow Time, there's something in there that I know I need. Up till now, my life has been rush, rush, rush. Finish something then on to the next. Eco is one thing – that kept my interest here long after I'd have got bored with another standard build. But Slow is one step further."

Caroline and Mikey were exploring upstairs. Dan took my arm and steered me out onto the deck. We sat at the outdoor table and he leaned towards me. "So tell me. Tell me all about it."

I struggled to find my voice again. "Really, I'm no expert. I've only just begun to look at it."

"But you've read, and you're a thinker, you're way ahead. I've heard people talk about Slow Food, but mostly pretty flaky types, or foodies who have no other passion. I hadn't heard of it in a wider sense. So tell me."

His eager face reminded me of my cousin's cocker spaniel, the way she would glue her eyes to mine when she thought a walk was in the offing. I felt myself relax, and a smile play on my face. "I'll tell you what I know. It's really not that much . . . It started with Dad's slow-cooker, like I said, and the *Slow* book – *In Praise of Slow* – but like I said, that was mostly about reacting against modern life, about not rushing, not prizing efficiency above all else . . ."

Caroline opened the door. "Cool, Dan, very cool. What next?"

"Can you and Mikey take yourselves off for a walk for a while? Jo and I have some things to talk about."

"Sure." Dan didn't see the expression on her face. He had turned back to me. I tried to ignore the taunting wave, the hyperactive eyebrows. She pulled the door closed behind her and disappeared. My embarrassment flared and died just as quickly. I resumed my train of thought.

"Like I said, I can see the appeal of turning away from that way of life. But it's reactive. I'm interested in something that is built from the ground up. So I started thinking, what are the concepts here? What are the values that designing life again from the bottom up can give us? I think that's what it is: starting from scratch. Thinking about what we'd want if we could have anything. So much of life is about expectations, and we don't always question them to make sure they still have value."

Dan nodded. "And? What did you come up with? You have a strategy? A new way to look at things."

"A strategy . . ." I turned the word over in my mind. I guess that was what I was working on, in between managing the necessities of life. And that was part of it, too. "I guess. The first thing is attending to the basics: Maslow's primary needs."

"Food, shelter, warmth, yes?"

"Yes. So with the town, the people who were struggling . . . look, I'm not sure . . . these are confidences, I don't want to say anything out of turn."

"In confidence, then, and just sketch it out – I don't need all the detail."

I hesitated again, working out what I could say. "For the people who were struggling, we put the basics in place. Made sure they had a decent place to live, and the means to maintain that. It's summer, so it's warm anyway. And then food. Dad moved his catering operation and scaled it up. He has a vision of running it commercially. I'm leaving it up to him after the fiasco . . ."

"Fiasco?"

"I offended him with my bourgeois assumptions and traditional thinking. He's got it sorted. He'll tell you about it himself."

"Okay. But go back. You're still talking about the fixes, survival. Tell me about the essence of Slow as you see it."

I looked out across the lake. I could still feel his eyes on me, and a warmth spread across my chest. I recognised a deep, soulful happiness. My body flooded with pure mountain air and I had the sense of sinking deeper into myself, of coming home. My smile flickered again, and for a moment I forgot the question, only to have it echo back through me as I replayed the sound of his voice. The essence of Slow.

"I think it's about going deep into yourself, asking yourself what you really want from life. We're not taught to do that, but the miracle of seeing someone in their flow, living their passion, is one we all recognise, and treasure, when it appears in front of us. I've started to imagine a world where everyone lives that way. So much of life is habit, assumption, and being busy because we assume that's how it is. What if we could just leave out everything that is not important to us; or better, start from doing nothing, and only take action when our hearts tell us that's what we must do to thrive? Look at me – born, grew up, did well at school, on to university because that's what was expected. Commerce was a surprise for most people around me, because they didn't know that was a thing, or what it was. I love business, the art and science of business. I'd watched people around me live from their own work . . . wait, that's off the track. What I need to say is, I loved that, but otherwise, I just followed a path, did the next thing that came up in front of me. Lectures, assignments, exams, work experience. Not looking out into the future, except when people asked me what I was going to do. And then, they were always offering me a plan, an idea – for me to accept or reject, it's true – I didn't feel compelled by pressure; but I didn't make any creative choices, either. Just one step in front of the other, with no vision. I want vision. I want to come up with something no-one's ever thought of before. I want magic, I want to express myself, uniquely, and create something huge."

I felt my arms rise from my sides as if I were about to launch from the deck and take flight. Then I remembered where I was, who I was talking to, and I blushed again. "I'm sorry. I don't know where that came from. I got carried away."

But miraculously, he was still listening, still eager. I felt he should be recoiling, running from the vague wildness of my dream.

"I told you. I haven't got it worked out yet. Not at all."

"And yet I'm getting something, seeing something. Feeling it. Tell me about your grandad. You mentioned him last night."

"Grandad. Where do I start? I thought he was a simple soul. We all did. Not too bright. But there was something inconsistent, because my grandmother adored him, and she was very intelligent herself. So I started watching him. Listening. Asking him questions. And there is some magic there, beautiful insights. Except I feel like I can't quite get at them. Like we're not quite fluent in each other's language. We all thought it was him who was out of step, but now I've begun exploring this new thing, Slow Time, Slow Life, I'm beginning to wonder . . ."

"What?"

"Wonder if it isn't him who has the answer. If it wasn't the rest of us who were out of step, all of us, up till now."

Dan nodded. My voice rang away across the valley and lake and faded. We sat in the silence, neither speaking, until Mikey's voice floated across to us, words of awe at the beauty and peace. Dan stood and I followed. He held his arm out to me and just touched my shoulder as we stepped back inside.

Together we watched Caroline and Mikey approach. We had one more minute alone, and I realised there was something more I needed to say. "There's another thing."

"Yes?"

"Change of pace is only one aspect of it, and not the most important aspect. Slow is a place to start, it creates a gap, a space for thinking, a point of perspective. But the truth of it, it's something bigger."

"What do you think it is?"

"I don't know. But I do know I've only just touched the surface. There's a long way to go." I stared at the ground at my feet for a second, then turned and lifted my eyes out across the wide space behind us.

"It sounds like a pretty fun journey."

"Yeah, I think it will be."

"I wonder, would you mind, would it be okay . . ?" But before he could finish his question, they joined us. It hung in my mind for the rest of the day. I looked for an opportunity to bring him back to it, to ask what he had wanted to ask me, but when it came, after dinner, in the lull between dessert and coffee when the others bustled and organised, and he and I were left at the table alone, my courage failed.

I turned to face him, and instead of opening my mouth to speak I found myself noticing the colour of his eyes, the edge of yellow surrounding pupils dilated in the candlelight, and maybe a little more from the excellent red wine. His tanned, smooth face brought me memories of magazine advertisements; the pastel yellow of his polo shirt and the thin white sunglass pattern against the tan spoke of luxury, of boats and skiing and wealth. I swallowed and my mood sank. He was out of my league. Forget it. Whatever he had been going to say this afternoon, the moment was gone.

SLOW TIME

28

Caroline came and bounced on the end of my bed. "Mikey's flaked out, snoring like a freight train. Can I bunk in here?"

"Sure."

"It was a fun day, huh?"

"Sure was."

"You like him, don't you?"

"Oh yeah."

"That's something new for you."

"Yeah."

I thought she would tease, wind me up, but I should have known better, Caro's always kind. She just looked at me fondly, a half smile on her face.

"How old is he?" The question was so quiet it was like it was trying to take itself back.

"He's thirty-four."

"Oh God!"

She tilted her head. "Don't worry about it."

"Don't worry about it!" I wailed. "Here I am falling for a guy for the first time in my life, and he's so far out of reach it's like, never going to happen. Wouldn't you worry if it happened to you?"

"It did happen to me. It happens to everyone."

"You've got Mikey. What are you talking about?"

"But you said first love. First love is always unattainable."

My curiosity distracted me for a moment. "So who was it for you?"

"You swear you won't tell?"

"Who? I thought you told me everything. I didn't know about this."

"You swear you won't tell? It would break Mikey's heart."

"I swear."

"Robbie Williams."

I drew a breath, waited for my expectant heart to quiet, then slammed her over the head with a pillow. "Fiend! Are you laughing at me?"

"Only a little bit. Shhh. Really. I do understand. But don't despair yet. He likes you."

"He's twelve years older than me and he's a god and a grown-up. He is never going to go for me."

Her eyebrows flicked upwards and she shrugged. "Well, there are no guarantees. But I've known him all my life. I wouldn't give up hope entirely."

I felt a warm bubbling in the pit of my stomach. "So what do I do? What do I say? Should I try flirting?"

Caro let out a shriek of laughter. "No! Just play it cool. Be yourself."

"How am I ever going to manage that?"

"You will."

"Will you help me? Take me out if I start making a fool of myself."

She just laughed again.

"Please? We'll need a code. If I'm drooling, or talking too much or whatever, you say, 'Anyone want a cup of coffee?' and I'll come out to the kitchen with you, and you can calm me down. Please?"

"Okay. Sure. Relax."

"You have to promise."

"Okay. I promise."

My heart settled down then. I even managed to feel happy at the thought of the next four days in his company.

We stayed in the next day. Russell, Viv and Dan were taking the boat out, but Caro wanted to stay back and read. Mikey got bored half way through the morning and we had the house to ourselves. I had found it difficult to settle, until finally I picked up the book Dan had been reading, a biography of Winston Churchill, and after just a few minutes I was lost in it, drinking in the details of another world.

"You know, he wasn't anything particularly special when he was young."

"No?" Caroline's amazing the way she can do two or more things at once. She carried on the conversation with me while still reading her own book, and occasionally texting other friends. I can only ever do one thing at a time. It's possible she wasn't really listening but if not, the act was convincing.

"He wasn't brilliant at school, or anything like that. He grew into it all, developed it himself."

"That's cool."

I continued my running summary as I read, relaxing more and more as the hours lengthened. Mikey came home and lay down on the sofa, his head in Caroline's lap, and appeared to fall asleep immediately. She stroked his head, continuing to read, text and agree with me, until the door opened once more, the sailors returned.

My heart jolted in my chest as Dan walked in. It was unnerving to have my body so far out of my control.

"I see I'll have to find something new to read," he said with a grin. Instantly I held the book out to him, blushing for the third time in two days. "No, that's cool. I'm going to take a shower, anyway, I won't need it for a while."

I coughed at the startling, instant image conjured by this statement. I said nothing, not trusting my voice. Various parts of my body heated like they'd been plugged into a wall socket. I shifted uncomfortably. Dan's eyes flared open and he flashed me another grin as he left the room.

I turned to see Caroline smirking. "Fancy a coffee?"

"Shut up."

Mikey opened his eyes and stared at me, perplexed. "I do, if there's one going."

Caro smiled down at him and made to slide out from under his head, but I couldn't sit still anyway. "I'll get it. How do you want it?"

"Cappuccino?"

"I'll have one too, thanks. Hot. Strong. Lots of foam."

I pulled a face at her. She knew exactly what I was thinking. That's the trouble with old friends.

Russell and Viv's New Year's Eve party started out fun, but I'm never really comfortable with excess drinking. I don't like to lose control myself, and I don't like it much when others do, either. Caro and Mikey were okay - I'm used to them anyway - but Viv was dancing on tables and several guests ended the night throwing up off the balcony. It was Dan who saved the evening for me, making sure I was supplied with soft drinks, steering away one of Russell's brothers who threatened to become too friendly.

"Thanks," I said, when he returned to make sure I was okay.

"No trouble. Uncles can be the worst for lechery. It's a sad thing."

I stared, trying to figure out if he realised what he'd said, then burst out laughing as he did. I searched for something to say. "You're a lot younger than Viv." Was that okay? How would he take it?

"I was an accident. Unplanned."

"Well, doesn't that just go to show."

"What?"

"Well, that . . . I mean . . . you know."

"No, tell me, what?"

He was teasing me. I really liked it.

"That thing about clouds and silver linings."

"Not sure my mum saw it that way."

"You can't be serious. I bet she adored you."

"What makes you say that?"

"Well, because you're . . ." I gestured towards him vaguely. I hoped he would put my ineptness down to the party mood.

"I'm what?"

151

"Well, you're . . . wonderful, lovely. Your mum must have been very proud."

"No regrets, you think?"

"I think not."

"Well. That's kind of you to say."

I bit my lip. Had I said too much? What did I have to lose, anyway? If I didn't let him know I liked him, I might not see him again. And he knew, anyway. We both knew he knew. He put an arm around me and steered me out onto the balcony. We stepped up to the railing and he pulled me towards him. Every place his body touched mine felt like it was on fire.

"It's beautiful here."

"Yes."

I felt him turn towards me. I couldn't bring myself to move. This was enough, right now. I didn't want to break the spell.

"Jo?"

I half turned my face, eyes glancing off his, suddenly earth-shatteringly shy. My lashes dropped. I looked at the ground.

He put a finger under my chin, pulled my face up so my eyes naturally lifted, too. I felt swallowed up in the darkness of his eyes, my last hold on myself anchored to the small points of reflected light as I shifted my gaze from one to the other and back again.

"I thought we might take a drive tomorrow. Take the Porsche and do that trip Caroline was describing, through the Haast Pass and up the Coast. What do you say? None of this lot will be up before noon."

I would have done anything, gone anywhere he asked. "Sure. That would be nice."

His hand went to my cheek. He leaned in next to my ear. "Set your alarm for six. We'll get an early start." The feel of his breath in the whisper sent a raging pulse through my body. I leaned into him, my eyes closing. I felt my breath, in and out, like there was someone else controlling it. He pulled back and I felt lips on mine. I froze. One second. Two. Then nothing. By the time I could convince my eyes to open he was gone.

SLOW TIME

29

Would he be there? Had he meant it? Would he remember? I was awake at four, and at five; at five thirty I couldn't stay in bed any longer. I got up, showered, put on the outfit I had selected last night, way too wired to sleep. I'd finished the Churchill biography, got to sleep around three. Two hours' broken sleep. Well, I wasn't going to be at my most articulate today anyway. Try to keep my mouth shut, avoid gabbling. That seemed like the best plan.

I crept into the kitchen and turned on the coffee machine. It sounded like a jackhammer, grinding the beans in the silence. God, I was going to wake the whole hung-over house. I stood still and waited. No movement. I let my breath out in a long, slow, full exhale and took the coffee outside, to the site of the kiss. I felt a wide smile bloom on my face as I closed my eyes again. The sun was up, shining full into my face. I felt totally, absolutely glorious.

An arm wound around me. "I love an early riser." Dan took the coffee out of my helpless hand and lifted it to his mouth. I watched, mesmerised, as he took a sip. "You ready to go?" I nodded. "Great. Let me grab some breakfast and we'll be off."

He heated a frozen croissant in the microwave. "Want one?"

"Not now. Maybe I'll take one with me."

"Good idea." He put in two more, pulling a paper bag from a drawer and wrapping them. I picked up my bag, ready on the sofa. I handed him his book, too. "Keep it if you want. I can read it another time."

"I finished it. Thanks, though."

"Good?"

"Yeah. Inspiring. I love to hear the story of someone before they were famous. Otherwise there's a sense that people are born different, that there's no hope for us common folk."

"But you think there is?"

"Maybe." I blushed again. What happened to my plan to keep my mouth shut.

He held the door open and we stepped into the garage where the Boxster sat shining next to Russell's four-wheel drive.

"You sure Viv won't mind?"

"I asked her. She said it was fine."

"When did you ask her?"

"Last night."

"And you think she'll remember?"

"No. But I left her a note. Come on. Do you want to go or don't you?" He held open the passenger door without waiting for me to answer. We both knew I wanted to go.

The garage door opened behind us. Dan's left hand rested on the back of my seat as he reversed out. It was a glorious day, sky blue, sun bright. Every colour seemed brighter, like the light-sensitive cells in my eyes had been turned up. I took a moment to explore what I was feeling and realised it was happiness, at an intensity I had never imagined possible. It occurred to me for a brief second that this might be it. This might be the high point of my life, right now, this moment, like the conception of bliss, the pinpoint start of a new life. Everything was different, everything was new, and so full of promise. This one cell could divide and divide and divide, bringing joy that I had never even known to want. I was in love, and at some level, in some form it was reciprocated. This was a miraculous instant of creation, something from nothing. Breath flowed through my nostrils: a miracle. Sun shone through the car window: another miracle. I turned my face to look at Dan, and the magnitude of this miracle threatened to burst my heart.

SLOW TIME

30

The road along the two lakes of Hawea and Wanaka is awe-inspiring. Depending on the cloud and angle of the sun, the water ranges from mid-blue to blue-black and back again; with wind the mood deepens and changes, whitecaps forming startling patches that reverse-echo the shade and shelter of the surrounding hills. Mozart's Requiem boomed from the speakers, perfect, perfect.

The car moved like it was glued to the road, the seat hugging my body, the sun glinting off the bonnet as we cornered towards the east. The road rejoined the northern end of Lake Wanaka, the view exploding dramatically even before I was fully aware we had left the water of Hawea behind, and at that moment Dan reached over, put his hand on my hand. I jumped, and he laughed.

"It's pretty great, huh."

"Wow, yeah."

There was nothing more to say and I let my thoughts wander unattended as I tried to capture the moment in memory, losing the joy and magic of it prematurely as I grieved it couldn't last forever. Ahead was the end of the lake. In minutes it was behind us and like a typical, spoiled New Zealand girl I rejected the grandeur of the encroaching mountains because they weren't the view I had left behind. Finally, as mist and cloud closed in, creating a feel of magic pre-history, I came out of my pout, and condescended to be impressed once more.

"Looks like we might get rain on the Coast."

I shook my head. "That's not possible. Not on my perfect day."

Dan's laugher rang again. Was I so witty? I loved that he was so ready be happy. And I was right; as we descended, the mist cleared, and as we broke out of the mountains onto the coast the cloud dispersed altogether, allowing unbroken sunshine.

I wonder, does the West Coast feel like home to every local girl? There is something about those wild, white waves that seems to pound out from inside me, not in from the outside. I breathed in deeply and forced every last atom of breath out, again and again, until I was high on oxygen. Now I was laughing, too. "This feels so strange, so foreign. I haven't had a real break, a real holiday, in I don't know how long."

"No summer vacations after exams were finished?"

"Working. Always working."

"No quiet semester breaks, skiing, tramping, anything?"

"No. Assignments. And more work."

"Till now."

"That was why I came home, to Folkstown. I was supposed to be working this summer, too, but I couldn't face it. After four years, I was done."

"I know that feeling."

"You're the same? Forgetting that it's normal to stop and regroup."

"Not so much now. But yes, when I was studying. And this build seemed to go on and on. You know how it is - scheduled to take six months, and actually takes nine, and the longer it gets overdue, the less you actually can take a break. My partners would have me there now, overseeing things while it gets established, but I put my foot down. Christmas is sacred."

"Where are they? Your partners."

"In the US. Queenstown prices have got to that point now, there aren't many locals who can put down that kind of money, take that kind of risk. Especially not with the extra costs the eco aspect involved. I was committed to that, and it helped with the consents, but I couldn't find local investment prepared to try it."

"What are they like?"

"Like? You mean, personally?"

"Yeah. Do you like them?"

"Sure. I admire their integrity, their principles. They're a bit daunting, though, so rich."

"Well, so are you. So are Viv and Russell."

"Not like this. You have no idea. Billionaires. I feel like a kid, like I'm four foot tall when I'm in a room with them. It's not their fault, don't get me wrong, they don't make me feel like that. But can you imagine? A few million would be nice, but I think I'd suffocate under the weight of a billion. It's unimaginable."

My thoughts drifted for a moment. Even millions seemed unimaginable; or rather, I thought I could imagine it, but maybe I was wrong. "I don't see the difference. Rich is rich."

"You think so? You can't just put a billion dollars in the bank and enjoy spending it. There's all this other stuff you have to know; investment, social responsibility. Anyway, tell me – how much money is rich?"

"I don't know. A million dollars?"

He shifted back in his seat. "Okay. So what would you do with a million dollars?"

I hesitated. He seemed wired, fascinated. I'd seen my physics teacher at school with the same look talking about Einstein's speed of light thought experiment.

"Look, I really don't know."

"Play along. It'll be fun." His smile was cute. I could imagine what he must have been like at nine or ten years old. "Go on. What would you do with a million dollars?"

"Retire? I don't know. Live a life of luxury."

"No! That's just it. If you thought you were rich with a million dollars, it would be gone in a year. You'd buy a house, have a few great trips to the supermarket . . ."

"Buy a car like this one . . ."

"Exactly. And then it would be gone."

"Well, ten million dollars then."

"Okay. With ten million dollars, if you were careful, you could be rich for a long time. Invest it well, a 10% return, even once you bought the house and the car, and you'd have a nice income. You could travel, relax. But you'd still have to think about it, make sure you didn't spend beyond your means."

"You're crazy. With a million a year . . ."

"Nine hundred thousand, once you'd bought the house."

"So, nine hundred thousand . . ."

"And then tax. Less than six hundred."

"I could move somewhere with a lower tax rate . . ."

"Oh, right. Rich and not able to live where you want. All that freedom."

"Okay, but even six hundred thousand . . . that's heaps."

"Less than two thousand a day. Easy to blow. Really easy."

"Okay. So I give up. How much do I need to be rich?"

"See, there's the question. Now it becomes, why do I want to be rich? You said you'd relax, do nothing, but that would drive you crazy. You'd either be suicidal or working again within three months, or two. So, rich lady. What are you going to do?"

I had no immediate answer. If my needs were taken care of, if I didn't have to work for money, what would I do? I realised this brought me back to exactly the same issues as the Slow question. What was important? What was my purpose in life?

"You see?" He was grinning wide now. "It all changes. When you're hungry all you think about is food. When you see a beautiful woman, all you think about is sex. When you have to think about the next dollar, you think that's the only thing you need. But it isn't. Once the dominant need is met, everything changes; the whole landscape becomes different. There is a whole new set of things to consider. That's why I was so interested. In you. In what you're doing. Because it gave me a different way to think about what I was already thinking about anyway. I'm so glad I met you. Jo? Are you listening?"

I was way behind. First the mind-bend of the ten million dollars, and more, and then I got caught up at the sex reference. What, if anything, did that have to do with me?

"Can you repeat the last bit? I went off on a tangent."

"The Slow thing. It gives a different perspective on money, on purpose, on life. I'm glad I met you."

"Oh." For a moment I thought the disappointment would overwhelm me. But I couldn't cry. Not here, in such close proximity. I turned and wound the window down. We were passing through a town – Franz Joseph, I think – so the breeze was manageable.

"What?" He seemed amused at my crestfallen expression.

"So that's why."

Now he laughed, a short, loud bark. He pulled over, turned to me, put his hand behind my head and bent it forward, shaking me slightly. "It's not the only reason. Did you think I didn't hear what I said? You are beautiful. And I am thinking . . . well, you know, what I said. But you caught my attention in this other way as well. It's a long time since anybody's done that."

I was silent, trying to untangle what he was saying, not sure enough of my analysis to rely on it. I'd just have to wait till he said something more.

"Come on. Are you getting tired of sitting? Let's have a wander, have a look at the town."

31

We had lunch in the Café de Paris in Hokitika, relaxing into two courses and coffee then strolling up the main street and through to the beach before heading back towards the car. Just before the café corner we came upon an old house, a bed and breakfast. Dan's feet slowed to a stop and the hand holding mine tugged me to him.

"That lunch was good, huh?"

"Yeah. Delicious."

"Makes me wonder what their dinner would be like."

"Well . . ." So obtuse. I didn't see where he was heading.

"I think we should try it. Find out."

"But won't that make us very late back?"

"Only if you consider a day late late."

"What?"

He pointed up to the window, to the Vacancy sign. "We could stay."

My mouth gaped open. Logic screamed 'too fast, too fast'. God, I'd never really even been kissed before yesterday, if you didn't count Jason, or the few boys who didn't really get that I didn't really like them. Not more than friends, anyway. I stared at him. I was so tempted. Terrified and tempted. What did it mean? Should I ask, or would that ruin the magic? If I asked, that didn't allow for the possibility that he didn't know, exactly, either.

"Okay." I heard the word come out of my mouth without consciously making a decision to say it. Should I take it back? I looked inside myself, felt for my gut. No, don't take it back. Go with this. It's magic.

We walked up the path and I hung back as Dan asked the owner for a room. Could she tell, that I'd only just met him, that this was happening so fast? Would she think I was a slut? My mind flew off, spiralling back on what I would think of myself if I weren't me. I had a wild urge to laugh, biting my lip as they worked out the details of en-suite or not (yes) and payment (credit card) and she led the way up to the room.

Then we were alone, and Dan's arms were around me, and after years of thinking and planning how I would do this, what I would think and feel and do, I just threw it all out the window and followed my heart and body and let my mind float free.

Lying still afterwards, staring at the ceiling, I felt around myself for any trace of regret. Not yet. That was good. Logic told me I knew too little about him. What was his past? I didn't even really know his present.

"It's probably a little late to ask this, but you are single, right? No wife or girlfriend I should have taken into account when I considered your invitation?"

"Single. Yes. More than two months now."

"And before that?"

"I had a girlfriend. And another before that. And another before that. Do you really want to know? It's pretty boring. Pretty standard."

"No, that's enough. Cute guy, successful, confident. It makes sense."

"So then, if we're not going to talk about that, what are we going to talk about?"

I rolled towards him and lay my arm across his chest. "Don't know. Don't care. Just happy." And I put my head down, closed my eyes and floated once more.

We woke early and walked on the beach again before breakfast. We had no luggage, nothing to pack, just the toothbrushes we had bought at the dairy the afternoon before. Back in our room we stood on opposite sides of the bed and looked at each other.

"Ready to go?"

"Yeah."

As Dan reversed out of the angle park in front of the gem shop I scrolled through Viv's iPod and flicked on Robbie Williams, smiling at the recollection of Caroline's confession. I leaned my head back and closed my eyes. "I want to live like Robbie Williams sings."

"And how is that?"

"You know, effortless, and full on. He hits those notes like they were there before he got there; it seems like he creates them straight out of his head, sublimating them rather than singing. You're almost surprised to see his lips move. And he's so happy, so happy when he's singing. I want to create the things I imagine that clearly, that effortlessly, that joyfully."

"You don't ask for much."

"But don't you think . . . don't you think the world would be a better place if everyone did ask for that?"

"I'm not arguing. Did you hear me arguing?"

I was easing into his company now, almost forgetting to wonder what came next, if anything. Another day and I would be heading home. The question hung over me, whether I would ever see him again after that. In this mood, in this moment, the answer seemed obvious: of course I would. There was no-one like him, and he was meant for me. And even as I thought it, some part of me recognised how fragile this confidence was, how soon it would vanish, like a child's soap bubble, when we were back in Wanaka, no longer alone. I blinked again, leaned back once more. "I want to live like Robbie Williams sings."

32

The road looked so different in reverse, coast and bush and the Pass and the lakes, all rolling backwards like an old home movie. Coming into town I closed my eyes, not wanting this to end. I opened them as the car rolled to a halt in front of the garage. It took me a moment to adjust, to start to grieve. We were back. I brushed away a stunned tear, and his hand came around the back of my neck again.

"It's okay, Jo, it's okay." He kissed me gently, then pulled back when the door of the house opened. Caroline. I'd always, always been happy to see her before.

Her parents appeared, Viv looking me up and down in a way I didn't really like, despite the apparent friendliness of her smile. And what must Russell think of me? He'd known me when I was three. We were pulled in different directions, each claimed by some of the others. I looked over my shoulder as Caroline took me downstairs, demanding details I wasn't ready to give.

"Come on! I tell you everything. You owe me after that cryptic text, and then not answering mine."

"I turned my phone off," I mumbled.

She was laughing, shaking her head. "Who'd have thought it? Uncle Dan's new trophy!"

"Don't say that! Don't!" I burst into tears, unable to bear the thought that that might be it, that it might all be over. I couldn't ask her what his pattern was, how long the others had lasted. For me this was so much more.

"Hey, it's okay." She tried to put her arms around me but I pushed her away.

"Not it's not! It's not."

"Are you worried what I think of you?"

My eyes opened wide and I glared at her. "What do you mean? If you don't know me . . . well enough . . . to know I wouldn't . . ."

Her eyes flared, too, and I saw horror in them. "Oh god, you're not . . . in love."

"Why not?"

"But Jo, it's Dan! You're so sensible. You wouldn't . . . Oh!"

My face felt cold. I flopped back, falling onto the edge of the bed. "What do I do?"

She sat down beside me, her arm around me, staring straight in front of her and absently stroking my hair. "It's okay. It's okay."

"Stop saying that! Everybody stop saying that." I started sobbing, a fierce emotional backlash against the abandoned joy I'd allowed myself to feel. How was I ever going to leave this room? How was I ever going to face him again?

Caroline broke the silence. "Well, come on."

"What?"

"Let's get back out there."

"Can't I stay here?"

She eyed me shrewdly. "You mean forever?"

"Maybe."

"No, Jo. The only thing to do is brazen it out. Come on, I'll get you a cup of coffee, we can just sit. Read a magazine. Whatever. But you can't stay here."

I knew that look in her eye. She wouldn't listen to argument. The only thing to do was stall. "Okay. But I need a shower first; some clean clothes."

"All right. But hurry."

"That's okay, you go on. I'll join you."

"Nah-uh. No way. I'll wait."

I glared at her and collected my clothes, hunting through for the top I knew accentuated my shape. Part of me hadn't given up yet, I realised. I stayed in the water for a long time, hoping Caroline would get bored and go up without me. Finally I heard the bathroom door open, the basin tap turn on. A second later the water went cold.

"Hey!"

"Get a move on."

"All right!"

I couldn't put it off any longer. Caro walked ahead of me and passed quickly through the living room to the kitchen. I stood at the door taking in the tableau. Mikey was at the table with Caro's laptop. Russell was lying on the sofa reading a car magazine. Viv and Dan were playing chess, their faces taut with competition. Dan looked up, gave a tiny flick of his head. I was pulled towards him like a magnet, like a fish on a line. When I got close enough he put out an arm, pulled me onto the arm of his chair. Viv grinned, showing teeth, but didn't look at me. She appeared totally focused on the board.

"You'll never win if you don't concentrate," she said, still not looking up.

"Life isn't necessarily entirely about winning."

"Let's hear you say that again when you lose."

I felt his arm tense, reacting against the suggestion, although his face stayed cheerful. It was a good act, would have fooled most people, but Viv just grinned again. Dan reached out and made a move. For the next twenty minutes the banter and goading traded back and forth. Only one piece was lost on either side. I drank the coffee Caro brought me, not looking up. I could see Viv better than Dan, and I watched her grin tauten, then fade. Dan's grip tightened around me; he played his pieces with his left hand, apparently nonchalant. The conversation slowed, then stopped, until finally, with a last move of his remaining bishop, Dan whispered "Check, mate." I wanted to cheer, but the silence was eerie. Viv's smile was just a few seconds late, her offer of a handshake stiff. When Dan took her right hand with his left, his right arm still around me, Viv's eyes flicked at me, a split second of hatred. Did she know how much I'd wanted him to win? Yes, and there was more than that, a layer of complexity I didn't understand.

"Don't cry, Sis. Listen, I'll make it up to you. We'll make dinner."

"We're having salad. All the ingredients are in the fridge."

"Simple then. You relax. Take some time for yourself."

She smiled again, teeth bare. I recalled a similar expression from a television documentary on primates, just prior to a fight.

"You're unkind," I whispered, once we were out of sight in the kitchen.

"She hates losing. It's funny."

"And I guess you'd have been a great sport about it."

He laughed. "It's just payback. She used to be awful to me when I was little."

"But why? Surely she'd have loved having a little brother. I know I would have."

"I was ten years younger. She'd been an only child. And I was an attention-grabbing little bastard." He laughed, at old memories. "She used to shut me in cupboards."

"Not really?"

"That's okay. I had my revenge."

"What?" My voice was breathy with fascination. He didn't answer, just laughed and kissed me, taking me by surprise.

"Come to my room tonight?"

I stared at him, every other thing falling out of my mind. "When?"

He turned away to hide the smirk on his face, opening the fridge door and starting to pull out lettuce, cheese, eggs. "Well, just an idea, but I was thinking bedtime."

I was glad he was facing away: my smirk matched his, and better.

SLOW TIME

33

My bag was packed and Caroline was getting the car out to take me to the bus.

I felt hypocritical thanking Viv, but I had a lot to be grateful for, and I wanted to say so. I also wanted her to ask me back. She waved away my inarticulate attempts, patting me on the shoulder. "You take care, Jo. Don't get into too much trouble."

Russell hugged me, and Dan walked me to the car. "I'll call you."

I watched him as we turned in the driveway, wondering if it were true.

"You okay?"

"Sure. You?"

"Very funny."

I didn't want her sympathy, so I changed the subject. "What about you and Mikey, Caroline, what's the future there?"

She smiled the smug, peaceful smile she reserved for the love of her life. "Marriage, kids."

"Anytime soon?"

"I think so."

I thought about this. "I've always wondered . . ."

"What?"

"What it is about Mikey? You seem so different."

"And you think that's a bad thing?"

I sensed I was treading on dangerous ground, but I continued anyway. "I just wondered what you see in him."

She went quiet. I thought she'd be angry. We pulled into the village car park, just along from where the bus would arrive and leave. "I love him like the sun and the moon. He's such a good man, and he loves me so deeply. He believes in me so strongly." She turned to me and her face was glowing like a Michelangelo. "Do you know what he's been doing? What he's planning? He's been selling my art. Taking it round the cafés and galleries and telling them to hang it, to sell it. You know how I am about doing that stuff myself – even the slightest hint of a rejection incapacitates me for days. He gets that. He says I should never have to face that. That I'm an artist and I should concentrate on my art. We'll be a team. If I'm a success so is he. And vice versa. So few artists make it. Even the good ones. Because they don't have someone to do that for them, and when they do it themselves it destroys them. I'm not strong."

"Yes you are."

"Not this way." Her expression hardened. "So, doubter! Is that enough? If I need a reason to love, and now you're an expert you'll know whether I do or not, is that enough of a reason?"

"Sorry. I'm sorry. I guess I'm just confused, and trying to make sense of things. It's a very good reason. If you need one. And I don't know if you do or not."

The bus pulled in. Caroline got out of the car and took my bag from the boot. "You going to see Dan again?"

"He said he'd call."

We looked at each other, her scepticism mirroring mine.

"It's okay. I'm not holding my breath. And I will hold myself together. I'm naïve, but I'm not an idiot."

She hugged me. "You know I love you. Call if you need me."

I stepped up onto the bus. "You, too."

I leaned my head against the glass, allowing the passing scenery to fill my mind, mesmerising myself by focusing on one distant point after another. My thoughts turned homeward, recalling my family and friends with a start of guilt that they had been so completely absent from my mind this whole week. At least I had something to do, a definite plan for when I got back. Having practical things to do would be my saving.

I had something definite to say to Jason, also. It had crossed my mind that what he needed was a reason to give up, and here I had it. I might not see Dan again, but I could still let Jason know about him. And then maybe we could see about finding him someone else, someone more his age. I breathed out a long breath. I was back in familiar territory, skilfully ignoring my problems by attempting to fix someone else's. The only difference was, now I knew I was doing it. I could no longer fool myself.

Grandad was there to meet the bus. I hugged him and let him take my bag. "Did you have a nice time?"

"Yeah. I did."

"What happened?"

"Oh, you know. New Year. Party. What did you do here?"

"Same as usual. How is Caroline?"

"Good. Can I tell you a secret? You have to promise not to tell anyone."

"You sure you should?"

"I have to. I'm bursting with it. I think she's going to get married."

A wide smile spread across Grandad's face. "That's very good. I'm glad she'll be happy."

Then a strange thought crossed my mind. If I was going to play matchmaker for Jason, should I extend it to Grandad as well?

I was looking at him in this new light when he spoke again. "So, when are we going to get started on these eco-pods?"

I blinked. "I thought we'd get everyone together in the next couple of days to talk about the next step. Why, what's the hurry?"

"It's time."

"But you always say there's no hurry, there's plenty of time." I was teasing him, gently, but he wasn't amused.

"No. Not always. Sometimes there's plenty of time, and sometimes it's just time. And now it's time."

I blinked again. As so often, I could feel he was right, could feel he knew something I didn't, and frustratingly couldn't grasp just what it was. "Okay, Grandad, okay. We'll get moving."

"Good."

I met with James, about the Slow City application. Mayor for a town the size of Folkstown is a part-time job; James was also the town's accountant, kind, with a heart of gold.

"I'm getting together everything we need. The more local enterprises we have, doing individual things, the better. We need to show we're encouraging them, keeping things local."

"What sort of things?"

"Everything from organic vegetables to hobbies and crafts. Anything where someone is doing what they love with a passion. The Slow Food idea is central, so the more we can show we are encouraging local ingredients, the better. We're lucky, around here that's not hard, there's almost everything we need already. I'm encouraging a few others to pep-up their hobbies – you know Minnie has that herb garden? I've convinced her to make it a small commercial operation. That'll look great on our application."

"Minnie?" I shook my head. "Do we want her in this?"

"It's time to forget that old stuff. Heal the wounds."

"She's a witch."

"Jo . . ."

"I hate her."

"You need to get past that. You need to be a grown-up, work with her."

"I don't want to."

"Jo . . ."

"All right! I get it. Let's move on. What else?"

"That's it, really. I'm going around everyone who has a hobby, something they make and could sell; finding ways to make them viable commercially. It helps our application, and it works, too. The more I look at it, the more it seems like a good way to live."

"And how soon can we make the application? I want to get that web-site up and going."

"One step at a time. Once we've got everything underway, there has to be a visit from a Slow City delegation. That will take time. Do the web-site, write something on there about the application, the intention. That'll give the search engines something to grab onto. Maybe we could even blog the process."

"Do you know how to do that?"

"It can't be that hard. I'll get someone to show me."

"Great. Perfect." I nodded. Something felt strange - good, but strange. "It's weird. I've never had this feeling before."

"What?"

"Delegation. Things happening that I don't have to do myself. I've always done everything myself before."

James smiled. "Like I said, this is my department. I am the mayor, after all."

"I didn't mean to tread on your toes."

"That's not what I meant. And I understand about delegation. You get more done this way."

"That's what I'm just figuring out."

Dad, Grandad and I sat over the final plans for the eco-pods. I had a clutching sensation in my chest and I had to work to keep my face neutral. "Are we really ready?"

"We really are."

"It seems such a big step."

Dad looked up from the plans. I felt his eyes on my face, but couldn't meet them. "Well, if we're going to do it, then it stands to reason we'll actually have to do it. Yes?"

"There's no need for sarcasm."

"What's up, Jo? This was your idea."

I jerked my head up and down in agreement, the movement dissipating some of my nervousness. "Yes. I know. It's okay. So where do we start? Do we have planning permission?"

"Yep. Dave at the council worked through the plans with us. We're ready to go."

I looked out the window at the large front yard, where we were building our prototype. I tried to imagine how the view would change, what it would look like from here. I realised the others were talking: logistics, deliveries of materials, timescales. Grandad sounded out-of-character practical, reeling off detail after detail. This was way more progressed than I expected.

"Did I miss something? How are we paying for this?"

"I took out a mortgage."

"When?"

"It got approved yesterday. What did you think? How did you think we would do it?"

"I was still working on that. I hadn't come up with a plan yet."

"Well, in the meantime, it's done."

"I don't like it, Dad. I don't like you taking my risks for me."

He blew out an exasperated sigh. "It's not your risk, it's our risk. It's not your town, it's our town. It's time you got over your delusions of grandeur and let everyone else take their part."

"But . . ."

"Jo, keep up. We're going to get this done. We need to keep moving forward, not rethink decisions that have already been made."

I did look into his eyes now. The texture of the moment was so familiar, echoing argument after argument over the years. We were well-matched, both self-righteous and stubborn. Now, as through the years, Grandad stepped in, putting out a hand to each of us, drawing us back to the plans. I had a fleeting moment of wondering how Dad and I would get on if he weren't here.

34

It was exciting, watching the foundations get dug, the pipes get laid for the sewerage. We had decided against the composting option – the world in general isn't yet ready to move away from the flush. I took the role of unskilled labourer in the working bee that followed. Everyone who had time pitched in, agreeing to swap labour for labour when their own turn came. My pride took knock after knock as I saw how much there was I didn't know, and as I watched the orchestrated process I was so far from having the knowledge and ability to manage myself. Yes, I had known this would be a team effort. But I hadn't been prepared for being such an insignificant part of it.

In four weeks that seemed much shorter, it was done. The electrician finished, handed over his orange sign-off sheet and Grandad flicked the light switch like this was another Christmas tree. Fifteen of us had gathered for this moment: Louise and Jason; Malcolm, James, Josie, Peter and others as well as me, Dad and Grandad. A cheer went up, and we all crowded inside the nearest half of the double pod. It seemed small, empty as it was. We were picking up the beds and sofas tomorrow from Timaru. As much furniture as possible was built in, to make the best use of space and save money on furniture. I slid onto the bench behind the dining table and watched the others milling around. There was a great sense of hope.

"Just need to get the guests now," said Louise.

"Bed first."

"Bed first," she agreed. "By the way, Jo, who is this guy Dan?"

My eyes goggled, blood draining from my face. "What do you mean? How did you . . ?" Jason was staring. I hadn't found a moment to talk to him yet – if I'm honest, I was putting it off, making excuses. I swallowed. "He's a guy I met at New Year. Who told you?" I wondered what she knew.

"Told me what? He's been sending us guests. We've had a whole run coming from some place out of Queenstown. They said Dan recommended us. So I thought you might know who he was." Her eyebrows raised. She hadn't suspected anything before, but she did now.

I cleared my throat. "He's Caroline's uncle." That sounded harmless enough. "He's done an eco development. He was interested in what we are doing."

"Well, tell him to keep it up, whatever he's saying. We've turned over $3,000 this week thanks to him."

Everyone looked around, eyes wide. "$3,000!"

"Uh-huh. You know something, Jo?"

"What?"

"I'm beginning to think this hare-brained scheme of yours just might work."

My heart was still beating fast, images of Dan competing with the attention of those in the room. In amongst it all, I felt something happen. People were smiling, excited by Louise's news, but also, indefinably, they had relaxed. It was like we had all been holding our breath and hoping, and here was the first piece of evidence justifying our faith.

"That's great, Louise. Really great news." I found another reason to smile, also. Dan hadn't forgotten about me. It wasn't over after all.

The next focus was marketing: the web-site, brochures for Louise's and the pod accommodation. We needed more guests, which meant attracting more people to the town, not just catching the ones who were coming through anyway. I knew I should call Dan, too, to thank him.

I decided to put it off until I was clear about what else I wanted to say, but then I found myself picking up the phone on a whim, and within twenty seconds he was on the other end of the line.

"Hey, Stranger."

"Dan. How are you?" My heart faltered a moment at the sound of his voice. Professional. Stay professional.

"Fantastic. Been meaning to call, but you know how it is.'

"Sure. I wanted to thank you for sending us those guests. I don't know if you know how much difference it's making up here."

"My pleasure. I know how it is when you're starting out."

"I've given Louise your details, web-site, etc. so she can return the favour. If you send me some brochures, we'll put them out. I'll give them to the tourist information office, too."

"Thanks. Appreciate it." There was a pause, a change of mood. His voice was slower, smoother. "So how've you been? What's been happening? I've missed you."

My breath trapped in my chest. It was a moment before I could answer. "Things are going great here. We've got the first eco-pod ready for guests, I just made up the beds today, and the next one's started. Seeing progress is keeping me sane."

"Got any guests booked yet?"

"No. It'll come, though."

"Well, if it's free tomorrow night, book me in."

"What do you mean?"

He laughed. "I mean I'll come up. Have a look. Pay to stay."

"I can't ask you to do that."

More laughter. "You didn't. And if it's necessary, book me in at your dad's restaurant. I told you I wanted to see it."

"You did. No reservation necessary, just turn up."

"And you'll join me?"

"Sure, I'll be there." I kept my voice light, wanting to make it clear I had no expectations, trying to keep my very un-cool girlish excitement a secret.

"Tell your dad I'm coming, ask if he'll find time to talk to me. I'll be there by two."

So easy. My day turned around in less than two minutes – the phone told me: our conversation had been one minute fifty three seconds long. I wrapped my arms around myself and gave up on the brochure I was writing. I skipped down the hall into the kitchen and danced around the table. No-one else was home. I picked up my keys and headed into town looking for company.

I was high, looking for anyone I knew to talk and laugh with. Louise's mother was outside the supermarket loading bags into her car. "Mrs Walters! How are you?"

"I'm fine, just fine. And how's the talk of the town?"

"I'm great, if that's who you mean. What are they saying about me?"

"That you're on fire with all those big city ideas."

I tilted my head, wondering if she was mocking me. Her eyes were sparkling, her expression kind. "Do they say I'm too bossy?"

"I don't care if they do. I was so worried about Louise, and she's happier now than she's been all year. You keep at it."

"I haven't seen you around. You should get her to bring you in to Dad's restaurant."

"No, you know me, creature of habit. I like a tomato sandwich for my supper, and a cup of tea afterwards. Nothing fancy like your dad would cook up."

"Well, but I could make you a tomato sandwich. And it's not just about the food. We get talking. Some of the old guys get to exaggerating, telling their day. It's fun. You're a bit of a storyteller; come down and spin us a yarn."

"Oh, now I haven't told a story since wee Jason was little. I can hardly remember how."

"And you don't keep the others at the retirement flats agog with the gossip?"

"Well, but that's different. People take an interest."

"Please, Mrs Walters. Tell you what, if you come tomorrow, you can meet a young man."

"One of yours?"

"One of mine."

She turned to a touch on her shoulder. I hadn't seen Jason approach. "Did you hear that, wee Jason?" He towered over her by nearly two feet. "Young Jo's got a young man."

I had meant to tell him, gently, quietly, away from everyone. But maybe this was better. He looked at me over his grandmother's head, his eyes asking a question, reading my answer. "Is that right? Well, Gran, you know I always know who to come to for the gossip."

"Gossip again! It's called news. Well, now, maybe I will come. You'll pick me up, Jason? I won't want to drive myself home at night."

All of three minutes in the car from the restaurant to the retirement flats, but Jason nodded.

"You're a good boy."

I smiled at him, trying to catch his eye, see that things were right. He avoided looking at me, his mouth straight and compressed, and pulled himself between me and the old lady. "Come on, Gran, let's get you home now."

"Don't forget, Jo, tomato sandwiches. And white bread. The other sticks in my teeth."

I wandered through the supermarket myself, recovering my light and celebratory mood. Dan's coming tomorrow. Dan's coming tomorrow. I wanted to buy something, spend money, totally frivolous. I ran my hands over the shelves as I passed. Not cake or chocolate or even wine. Ah, here we are: candles. I chose a selection, bought a box of extra long matches, just because they were there. I didn't know how much time there would be for romance, or whether Dan's thoughts were even turning that way, but mine were, and I had a wile or two, a trick or two up my sleeve, naïve though I was. The sun glanced through the large front window of the store and I caught sight of my shadow on the floor, long, slim and sexy. I tried a model's walk, hips swaying. I could do that, as long as I didn't start to laugh.

I picked up a new body spray, testing the varieties for fragrance. My eyes settled on the floor as I waited at the checkout. Time to go home for a makeover, get myself ready for love.

SLOW TIME

35

I was so shy when Dan arrived. So shy. I couldn't look him in the face. He put an arm around me and laughed. Dad looked from one of us to the other and back again. Maybe I should have warned him that this was how things were.

We put his bag in the pod and he looked around, commenting on where it differed from his build, and where it was the same. He was gentle with Grandad as he asked questions, their language becoming a lyrical dance. He had Caroline's gift for appreciating people, losing that sense of mischief I sometimes felt directed at me. I pouted for a minute, until he reached over and put a hand on my face, questioning. I hadn't thought he was paying any attention to me, and forced a smile to cover my chagrin.

We walked around the streets, Dad pointing out where the rest of the projected pods would go. Peter's was already underway, and the boys looked at the holes in the ground for way longer than they interested me. I stood back, watching, enjoying the way they talked. They would get on well. After a bit, Dad stepped back, wiping his hands on his trousers.

"Time for me to get cleaned up, get cooking. We'll see you tonight?"

"You will."

"We'll be there around six." Dad was walking away. Remembering Nancy, I ran after him. "Nancy Walters is coming in. I said I'd make her sandwiches, so if she gets there before me, let her know I haven't forgotten, will you?"

"And you're sure you won't forget?"

"What do you mean?"

His eyes narrowed. "He's a charmer. Good looking. A great deal older than you. You won't get distracted on the way?"

I put my hands on my hips. "I will not. Are you suggesting I can't look after myself? That I don't know what I'm doing?"

"Did you need me to tell you? You know it yourself."

I wanted to be angry, but instead I burst out laughing. Dan and Peter turned, and I lowered my voice to answer. "You are so lucky I'm in a good mood."

"All right, then," Dad said, as he turned away, then quietly, under his breath, not meant for me to hear: "Long may it last."

Made-up, dressed with care and sparkling with happiness I was dazzling that night. I felt many eyes on me, and I loved it. Dan was witty when he spoke, but said little, listening with great attention to those he chose out of the crowd.

Nancy challenged the old boys with her glee and spiky turn of phrase, drawing us all in, one by one, to the circle that formed around her. She kept looking at her watch, saying it was past her bedtime, smiling at the protests and spinning out one more story, and then another.

Jason didn't join us until after nine, looking over with a sour expression at Dan and me, sitting close. Something was off about him. I thought he might have had a drink or two, but not enough to make him unsteady on his feet, or embarrass himself. I stood up when he made to drive Nancy home, however, whispering so no-one else would hear.

"Are you okay to drive?"

He sneered at me. "Yes, Mum, I think so."

"No, you're not."

"What are you going to do? Make a scene?"

"If I have to. But not if I don't." I cleared my throat. "Peter, would you run Nancy back? I need to talk to Jason."

Jason opened his mouth to protest, but I shot him a poisonous look. Don't push it. "Here, come outside."

"What is it?" he said, once the door had closed behind us. "Want to give me a kiss without Lover Boy seeing?"

"That's right, Jason. I didn't fancy you when you were sweet and kind, but this nasty side is a real turn-on."

There was a moment when the situation was outside my control, when I had no idea which direction he would take next. Would he lash out? Would he crumble and cry? I held my breath, ready for whatever came. He turned and walked away, his movement angry rather than dejected. I watched him, wondering which I would prefer.

The door opened. Peter came out, with Nancy, wrapped against the summer evening in a long woollen coat. I opened her car door, not noticing Dan come up behind me.

"Did I tread on somebody's toes?"

I said nothing as Nancy tottered in, falling into the seat, reaching back for her safety belt. I waited until the door was closed, goodbyes said, the car pulling out before I turned.

"I know how you like competition."

"Call that competition?"

"Ooh! That's not gentlemanly. He's just a boy. You could have the grace to . . ."

"What, give him a head start? Bow out to see if he can charm his way into your heart? Actually, you know what? I think I'll use whatever weapons I have to to win."

"Win what?"

"The fair lady's heart."

I tried to stop myself from laughing and failed. A delighted giggle escaped me. "I foresee this as very entertaining."

"As the lady wishes, it shall be done."

36

Dan brought out something new in me, a physical confidence, a hint of the siren. In response to a raised eyebrow, a suggestive tilt of the head I sneaked into the house, picked up my toothbrush and a long t-shirt and stepped back out into the dark.

"Dan? Are you there?"

He moved into view from the porch, triggering the sensor lights. "I was just watching the stars. You all set?"

"Yeah." My voice was breathy. I noticed my shoulders were pulled back, my chest lifted. God, I was so obvious, and such a cliché. I didn't care, just laughed into the half-light.

Dan pulled the cork from a bottle of wine, poured into two of the large glasses I had just the day before stocked into a cupboard. I felt so grown up, gazing at him over the top of the glass, sipping as if I enjoyed it.

"You've done well. Are you proud?"

"Of what?"

"Of this." He gestured around him.

"This wasn't me – I'm only manual labour in this side of things."

"But it wouldn't have happened without you. It's your vision, your courage."

"Well, it had to be someone's." I shrugged. I didn't really want the credit, and the responsibility that came with it.

"Your dad's a bit of a visionary, too. I've never felt anything like that restaurant, and I've been in a lot of places. It is something totally new."

"Yeah. He's unique and he knows it. A prima donna. Don't encourage him."

"But why not? What he's created is highly marketable, if we can reproduce it. A potential gold mine."

"Well, but how many places do we need? It's a small town."

"I wasn't necessarily thinking about here. But the town will grow. I see lots of potential."

"But do we really want it to? The idea was to keep what we have alive, to make the people happy, to give them back their lives. Beyond that . . ."

"Beyond that there's so much potential. The world is hungry for Slow Living, and you have the elements of it totally down, fitting together. You've created something special."

"It's not finished, and it's not . . ."

"Not . . ?"

"It's about the people, about facilitating life. Not profit. Not expansion."

"Even if you have a gift to offer the world?"

I was stunned into silence. This was a new direction of thought, a bigger picture than I'd imagined. I had hardly caught up with where we were.

"Listen, I'm looking for a new project. The Queenstown development is finished, handed over, all but. I'm just hanging round now, less and less useful. My partners have been over, had a look, they're stoked, and they want me to do something new. Something different. I think this is it. I think what you've done is the start of something I could finish, bigger than your wildest dreams."

"But how . . . how would it be? What would it mean?"

"I don't know yet, but I'm excited, I have ideas flowing like a river. We could talk them through, I love the way we bounce off each other, when we get on the same track of invention."

His eyes were glittering with creator's madness. I knew that look, I'd often had it myself, but I didn't like it. It didn't feel right. This wasn't just a project, it was real life for my family and friends. These decisions weren't mine, and they certainly weren't his. "I don't know. Once we get the money flowing, maybe that's all we need. The people are happy, in general, in the background. Too much change is dangerous. It can upset things. It's uncontrollable, unpredictable."

"I didn't think you'd be a wet blanket. You have so much imagination, so much courage."

"Courage for what I know is right."

"And who says this isn't right?"

"I didn't. But I just don't know."

"It's progress. It's inevitable. Growth or failure. You know that. Business is always growing or fading."

"This isn't a business. It's a town."

"Which you've made into a business, a co-operative business, in order to save it."

"That's not exactly . . ."

"Look, I know it's scary. But we can talk, can't we? Plan. Scheme. Follow through the thought experiment and see where we end up. There's no harm in that?"

"I suppose not." I lifted my shoulder, rubbed it against my cheek. "But I've missed you." I walked over and put my hand on his shoulder. He reached up and took it in his, pulling me round and down onto his knee. "Couldn't we talk later?"

He didn't answer, pulled my hand to his lips now, then moved his mouth to my neck. I reached for the remote control and dimmed the lights so that our shadow reached darkly towards the bed. As my thoughts shut down I caught a fleeting glimpse of the future as he'd suggested it, a busier bustling town. It felt twisted, unfamiliar, just for a moment; then it was gone.

37

I woke to the sound of the door opening and closing. Dan turned, wearing just a towel, holding a breakfast tray: croissants, jam, juice. Two glasses. I squirmed with embarrassment. What must my father think of me?

"Hungry?" The word vibrated out of Dan like a growl.

"Yes. But I'm still sleeping. Come and wake me up."

He put the tray on the table and came over to the bed, sitting down, leaning over me. "Morning," he purred. My lips stuck to his, dry from sleep. I wet them.

"Hi." I leaned back against the pillows, pulling him into me. He kissed me once more, but his body resisted the tug of my hand. "You're preoccupied. What is it?"

"I've just been working things out, thinking things through." He gestured towards a mess of handwritten notes on the desk. "Come on, get up. I want to brainstorm with you."

Despite the interruption to my morning languor, I liked this high energy mood in him, and the fact that he was so eager to hear my ideas. I reached out and pulled on the shirt he had been wearing yesterday. As I stood it fell fluidly to my mid-thigh. Perfect. Just the right mixture of alluring and business-like.

"Just let me take a shower."

"No, now. I've been waiting for you to wake up."

I laughed at the childish pout. "Okay." I poured myself coffee from the cafetière, added milk and leaned into the rear banquette, pulling off the claw of a croissant. "Bring it over here, so I can eat as well as talk."

He shuffled the papers into a loose pile and dropped it in front of me. I brushed some crumbs off the table, but he was unconcerned. "I've been beginning another thought experiment, about Slow Time. I think there's way more to it than we've discussed yet. I think there are lots more elements that we could add to the town, if we think it through properly. So tell me what you know."

The question took me by surprise, but he was waiting, expectant. I took another sip of coffee and combed through my thoughts. "Slow is about going back to natural rhythms. Seasons. Hours of daylight. It's about knowing what's important to you as an individual, and knowing how that fits with the community. It's about doing things on a comprehensible scale, and with values thought out and embedded in every activity. It's about being present in the moment and not rushing on to the next thing. It's about being conscious: making conscious decisions, seeing what's happening around you. It's about using the senses - all of them - and the more I think about it, the more I realise that means more than just five - there are gaps in just the five - the awareness of the body, where the various parts are in relation to each other; awareness of energy in the body; awareness of how people around you are feeling. All those things are about where you direct your attention."

"What do you mean?"

"Let me try to explain – but I don't fully know yet what I'm talking about. There hasn't been much time to think, and I keep getting distracted by emergencies, or things that need to be done . . ."

"I don't care. Try. Tell me."

"Well, let me give you an example. Have you ever had the experience that someone is asking you for something, and it doesn't make sense? It seems random, unnecessary, but you can see they really do need something. Do you have an example of that kind of thing in mind?"

Dan frowned. "Yeah. My mum used to do that, all the time. So?"

"So, what did you do about it?"

He swallowed, disquiet crossing his face. "Ignored it as much as I could. Delayed, avoided. I felt really guilty about that when she died."

"Hey . . . sorry . . . we can leave this."

"No. Go on."

"Or maybe find another example."

"I said it's fine. Let's work with this one."

"Well, look back, and let your mind go. Ask yourself the question: what did she really want? What did she really need that she didn't know how to ask for?"

"Attention?"

"Be more precise."

"Well . . . she wanted me to get her, to understand her . . ."

"And how do you know?"

"I don't know. I just know. God, and I just brushed her off."

I reached out and pushed the hair back from his forehead. "Don't worry. It happens. I'm sure she forgave you. She knew you loved her . . ."

He stared ahead, eyes unfocused. I waited a beat or two before continuing. "That thing, that 'just knowing' – where do you feel that?"

He looked towards me again, gaze settling on me. He gestured vaguely around the top half of his torso.

"It's like a physical feeling, right? A sense? That's what I mean. The same as if you close your eyes and know the position of your arm. The same as if you ask yourself how awake you are, whether you feel up to running a marathon, or even if you have the ability to concentrate on some wild new pointless train of thought."

"It's not pointless. Keep going."

I closed my eyes. "Where was I? Okay. So Slow is about tuning in to all those things, in the moment. About focusing on the current thing rather than being distracted by the next."

"So you're saying you can't plan?"

"No, of course you have to plan. But then planning is the thing you're doing. You focus on that."

"But executing a plan means doing the first thing, then the second, then the third. You're always thinking about the next thing, because what you're doing now feeds into it."

"That's one way of working, but it's inefficient. It makes way more sense to keep the intention in mind and let the next action grow out of the previous one after it's complete, or as a natural insight while it's in progress."

"I don't understand."

"Try a little harder."

"Witch! Explain."

"No. You think."

"So let me get this straight . . . you don't make detailed plans, you just do things when the moment feels right?"

"That's the ideal."

"How can that possibly work?"

"I don't know how it works. You have to try it, experience it for yourself. And I'm only a beginner at it, I still battle with my control-freak ways."

Silence. His face flexed and shifted with each passing thought.

"Another aspect is to let the environment, the circumstances, dictate. It's night: sleep. It's dawn: wake. You're hungry: eat – if it's summer: eat strawberries; if it's winter, roast vegetables. And in winter, rest, conserve energy, contemplate. Be active when the weather encourages you to be active. And then comes the final thing, the hardest thing."

"Which is?"

"When there's nothing to do, do nothing."

"And how do you know?"

"Again, trust. But that last thing is the one that makes the difference, that stops mindless action, like shopping for entertainment, like any compulsion. If there's nothing to do, do nothing."

Silence again. I was done. Almost. I left a pause of another minute or two, then said, "I read a quote the other day, I don't know who said it, but here it is: faith isn't blind, it's visionary. That's how you do it. You create the vision. Then you trust."

I got up then, swallowed the rest of my coffee, headed for the shower. The feel of the water on my body was gorgeous. I closed my eyes and relived scenes from last night, Dan's slow, confident movements, my scattered expectation, delighted and thwarted time after time. I took my time, washed my hair with the luxurious shampoo I had spent over half an hour selecting, not guessing I'd be the first to experience it. I cringed as I thought of Dad, of Grandad, knowing I was here, not knowing what to think. They'd never had to deal with this idea before. Grandad would be fine with it, I was sure, but Dad . . . things had been strained enough, with the rebalancing of power through the recent projects. I felt for that sense I had described to Dan. What did Dad want? And the answer came, from that deep sense within me: freedom. Freedom? What the hell did that mean?

Frustrated, I turned off the water and stepped out of the shower, pulling a fresh, warm towel off the rack. I rubbed my hair, too hard and tied the towel around myself. I realised I had no fresh clothes out here. That was an oversight. I pulled yesterday's outfit back on, feeling vaguely sleazy.

38

Dan was still madly sketching and writing, this time buildings, maps, clocks.

"What are you doing?"

"It's all great, what you said. Fantastic. People will love it. It's totally new. So now for the practical aspects. We can attract a lot of people with a full exposition of the philosophy. I'm looking at how we can house them, feed them, what else we can offer."

"But the pods . . ."

"Fine, but much too small scale. One unit per home! Hopeless, once things really get off the ground."

"That depends how fast things grow, surely."

"The faster the better, I'd have thought."

"Did you listen to me at all? This is about Slow."

"But you said yourself, Slow doesn't have to be slow. It just has to be considered, conscious – visionary." He gave me a cheeky smile, like the one he had given Viv when he beat her at chess. My nose twitched into a momentary sneer.

"I have a vision. And it's not this." I picked up the top three pages and dropped them again. One of them fluttered onto the floor.

"What's wrong with this?"

"Ill-considered."

"Because I came up with it fast? Remember, I've done developments before. I'm ahead of you on a lot of things. I can think faster."

"Tchah!"

"Calm down, Sweet. I didn't mean any offence."

"You don't know anything about this town, or the people, or what's best for them."

"I met them last night. Great bunch. Energetic. Intelligent. Ready for more."

"These are deep relationships, formed over generations. You can't introduce hundreds of incomers overnight and expect the atmosphere to survive."

"Of course it will survive. They'll adapt."

"They'll be overwhelmed. Everything will change."

"And you don't think they're ready for that?"

"Ready for it! What are you talking about? What do you think the point of all this is?"

"Progress. Creating wealth."

"No! It's about preservation. Saving something that was threatened with extinction."

"The only way to resist extinction is to evolve."

"Evolution is slow."

"Not always."

"People need time to think things through."

"Are you sure you know what's best for them? Your father thinks you're being overbearing, taking too much on yourself."

"Fuck off! What do you know about my father and me?"

"I just listened when he talked. Have you tried it?"

"Shut up!"

"Are you really so sure you know what's best for them?"

"Change needs to be thought about, properly, not just arbitrarily gone ahead with." My head was beginning to spin, my argument coming full circle. I couldn't think clearly.

"We will think it through. These are just ideas. Just a start. Sit down. Let's work on them together."

I shook my head. "I need some air. I'm going for a walk."

"I'll come too. We can talk."

"How can you be so calm when we've just fought like this?"

"Fought? What do you mean?"

He seemed really not to know. The argument had put me severely off balance. He seemed just as calm as always. Even a little smug.

"Look, I need some time alone. To think. I'll be back, soon."

I pulled the door behind me, cutting him off mid-sentence, and began to walk. I wanted to be away from Dan, but my own thoughts were still in a spiral. I headed to Josie's for a dose of her down-to-earth sanity.

SLOW TIME

39

I found Josie gardening, kneeling by the gate pulling up weeds.

"Hey there."

"Hey, Jo. How are you?"

I sat down on a stump close by, hunching up my shoulders, digging my hands deep into my pockets. Josie sat back on her heels, watching me, waiting for me to speak. The silence lengthened. Finally she leaned forward again and continued weeding. My thoughts spun around each other, making only transitory, shifting sense.

"Good-looking fellow, that Dan."

I smiled, feeling a buzz move through my chest; too soon it was gone, replaced by unfocused anxiety.

"Nothing's clear any more."

She sat back again, waiting, then stood and gestured inside. "I'll make some tea."

I followed her idly with my eyes as she moved around the kitchen. When the mug appeared in front of me I stared into it, watching the wobbling, distorting reflection of the room and me in it.

"Nothing's clear any more."

"What's not clear?"

"What to do. Dan wants . . ." My thoughts wandered again, picturing the vision he had painted. I saw him walking in and out of the buildings, smiling vaguely at his graceful stride. I tried to bring him into the town streets, also, but the picture didn't work so well here. I frowned. Josie cleared her throat. I looked up, startled. I had forgotten where I was. "I'm sorry. What was I saying?"

"What does Dan want?"

"He wants to build a big development, grow things fast. I'm not so sure."

"You're a thing, you and he?"

"Yeah."

"Serious?"

"I've no idea."

"You think that might be the source of your confusion?"

"What?"

"Seems to me you're mixing two things together. Separate, they might seem less complex."

My chest constricted. I jutted out my jaw, bit on my upper lip.

"If someone else came to us and talked about a big development, what would you do?"

"Talk about it. We'd all talk about it. Decide what to do."

"So why's it different because it's Dan?"

"Because I brought him here."

"And you'd like him to stay?"

"Well . . . I've never had a boyfriend before. I don't know if I want him to stay. He makes me feel . . . off-kilter."

"But happy?"

"Yes. Sometimes. Most of the time. Except when he laughs at me."

Josie nodded. "I think you need to get that sorted first, Kiddo. The other part will wait. But if you don't want him around, you don't want him around."

"I didn't say that."

"Didn't you?" She frowned. She looked worried. "This is one you need to decide for yourself. Only . . ."

"Yes?" I was hopeful she was going to give me some clue, an answer, so I'd know what to do.

"You're being careful, aren't you? Being safe?"

I sighed. I wanted to cry with disappointment. "Yeah. We're being safe."

I stood up, put my hands back into my pockets and pushed the chair in by hooking my ankle around one leg and scraping it across the floor. The door was open. I swung stiff legs from side to side, leaping lightly down from step to step. My shoulders slumped as I mooched along the footpath. Was this supposed to be love? It felt awful. One second I felt a flutter in the pit of my stomach as I remembered a glance or a touch. The next it had turned sour as I heard his mocking laugh, his competitive taunts. I couldn't love someone I was in competition with and I couldn't compete with someone I loved. But Dan was different. It seemed he was built different from me. Unless he didn't love me. Unless I was nothing to him at all.

SLOW TIME

40

He was still at the table. Still drawing, still making notes.

"What are your intentions? What are your plans for you and me?"

He looked up, a knowing smile on his lips. "I wondered when that was coming up. I don't really have any intentions. I usually just wait and see where things go. I'm sorry if that upsets you."

"I'm not upset." And oddly, I wasn't. "I'm just deciding what to do."

"Look. Come here. We make a great team, you and I. You have some great ideas. A sexy mind."

I rolled my eyes, tossed my head back, my hair flowing.

"You're not like anyone I've ever met before. You just need to loosen up a bit. Enjoy the experience."

"Do you know how much of a bastard you are in this mood?"

"Please, come sit down. I'll try to behave."

I wavered. He had a different side, I knew it. He'd been such great company when we drove down the coast, when he wasn't so intent on winning. "No. Forget it. Forget us. That's it." I turned and walked back to the house, straight to my room, closing the door behind me. Confusion and grief crashed around me. I put my head under my pillow and cried.

Hours later Grandad knocked on the door and came inside. "Jo? You okay? You didn't come for dinner."

I lifted my head. At the sight of my red and swollen eyes his face crumpled, tears forming. "Oh, Jo. What happened?"

"It's Dan. I broke up with Dan. Except I don't know if you can break up if you've never . . . had a commitment. Anything explicit."

He rubbed my back. "It's all right, Jo. It's all right. But I don't understand. Dan was there. He was very happy. Laughing. Telling us all his grand ideas. Isn't it great, about the hotel?"

"What?"

"He told us. About the hotel. He said you'd been planning it together. He didn't say you'd broken up."

"Well, but . . . what did everyone say? Do they want it? Don't they think it's too big? Too much, too fast?"

"It's only two hundred people. The town can cope with that. Dan said."

I sniffed, frowning. Thinking. Two hundred people. In a town of 12,000 that wasn't so many. I half rolled over, propping myself on one elbow.

"It's all Slow, you see. He was asking and asking about Slow. I like him, Jo."

"Do you really? What do you like about him?"

"He's kind. He's funny. He's quick. Like you."

"But he's . . ."

"And he likes you. He appreciates you."

"He said so?"

"I can just tell by the way he talks about you."

"But he's not like you, Grandad. He's complex. He's changeable. Sometimes he's not very nice."

"Well then, Jo, you tell him. Maybe he doesn't know how to behave."

I gave an involuntary laugh. He might just be right. I suspected Dan's girlfriends before now had been lightweights, bimbos. Maybe no-one had ever told him he was out of line.

"He's still here?"

"He's in the kitchen, having a cup of tea with Dad."

I tilted my head. I could hear the murmur of voices. I wiped my hand over my face.

"Why don't you come out?"

"Okay. Just give me a minute."

Dan looked up when I came in, with such a touching look of sorrow and remorse. "Sorry," he mouthed, when Dad turned towards me.

"Where have you been all day? We expected you at dinner."

"I'm sorry, Dad. I had some thinking to do."

"Well, let me get you something now."

"It's okay," Dan interjected. "I'll do it. There's still bread, tomatoes, cheese in my room. Can I make you a sandwich?"

I nodded, resisting the need to sniff. "Okay. Okay, Dad?"

"Yeah, sure, whatever." His voice was tetchy, but he had the same expression in his eyes as Grandad and Josie. Like when I fell off my bike, or when I announced some grand ambitious plan. Like when they wanted to protect me, and knew they couldn't.

"Thanks. I'll see you tomorrow, okay?" I hesitated a moment and leaned in to kiss him on the cheek, then followed Dan out to the pod.

"Grandad said you told them. About your plans."

"Our plans. Please. They like it." His eyes narrowed. He was watching me closely, trying to work me out. "Listen, I'm sorry. I didn't mean to be rude. Can't we just get over it, get back to where we were?"

"Only if we set some ground rules. You just can't talk to me like that. Like I'm an idiot. It can't be win or lose between us. It's got to be co-operation."

He tilted his head, perplexed.

"You like to win, right?"

"Right."

"So okay, I get that. But you treat me with respect. Compete with someone else. Or that's it. I go."

"But . . ."

"I mean it. I like you, God, you can be so lovely. But I won't be treated like a fool or a plaything."

He blinked, at a loss for words.

"Deal? Or I'm gone."

No answer. I turned and reached for the door.

"Okay. Deal. Jo, don't go." He put his arms around me. "Am I really a bastard?"

I laughed. "You are really a bastard. Sometimes."

"Well, then. Just, you have to let me know. So I know. I know I can change."

"We'll see."

"No competition? Really? Won't you get bored?"

"No. But you might. So we'll have to keep you occupied some other way. Channel that competitive nature somewhere else, somewhere appropriate. Into business, or sports? How about sports? Do you like tennis?"

"Yeah, sure."

"Well, tomorrow I'll introduce you properly to Jason. I have a feeling he'd be glad to have an opportunity to beat you . . . I mean, play you."

"Okay. And in the meantime," he bent his head and kissed me on the neck, "I can work on being lovely."

I closed my eyes, body relaxing and tensing in ever-shifting patterns. "Yes. Work on that."

SLOW TIME

41

As predicted, Jason thrashed Dan at tennis. I took shameless delight in watching each point, Dan throwing himself fully into the game and around the court while Jason laconically flicked the ball to wherever Dan wasn't. Despite the sweeping loss, Dan kept up his charm, his playful banter, pretending not to notice when Jason glanced over at me in triumph. At the end of the game he suggested a re-match, this time mini-golf. I kept out of arm's reach, trailing behind as they sauntered along the road to the course. I wouldn't let Dan take his revenge by playing up his advantage with me.

At the beginning of the game the boys were fairly evenly matched in ability, the only difference being in temperament: Dan was still feigning unconcern; Jason was unable to conceal his need to win. He lost on the second hole and his face became tense and determined. Dan just leaned on his club and kept talking. Jason's replies became shorter and shorter, finally reduced to aggressive grunts as he tried harder and harder and did worse and worse.

I felt bad for him, but it was comical to watch, at first. Then something else began happening. In the same casual voice, with the same light charm, Dan began a new topic: the hotel development. Innocent enough, vague and sketchy at first. Jason looked up with interest, then concern. Dan called his attention back to the game – it was his shot – and kept talking. Jason was more and more distracted, more and more upset. He turned to me, just as Dan finished talking.

"But what about the guest house? What about Mum? What about me?"

"We'll give you a job if you want one, your mum, too, if she wants. There'll be plenty of work for everyone," Dan continued blithely.

"Jo? Is he talking rubbish, or what?"

"Of course I'm not talking rubbish. We'll be starting the build in a couple of months, all going well. Jo's got a good head for business, she'll be my number two."

The club fell from Jason's hands. "Was this why you called me? So you could land this on me?"

"No, Jason, really. Shut up, Dan! Nothing's set yet. Nothing's decided."

"So you were going to decide it all, and then tell us. Your little puppet of a town. Think you can make us all dance when you want to? Well, we have so far, but that was for you, not your jumped-up boyfriend with his creepy looks and his gay shoes."

Dan glanced down, then recovered. "It'll be good for everyone."

"Shut up! I'm not talking to you! Jo, why?"

"Just wait. Let me explain."

"No. I'm sick of listening to you talk. I'm going home."

I made to follow but Dan held me back. Jason was too fast anyway. I slumped, turning away to hide my frustrated tears. "Why did you have to do that?"

"You didn't seem to mind when he was beating me."

"That was different. This isn't a game."

"Life's a game, Sweetheart. Didn't you know that? You told me I could compete in business or sports. This is both. Or have your rules changed again?"

"Don't you care at all about how people feel?"

He frowned, honestly confused. "He's a poor loser. It'll do him good to learn."

Boys. I wrapped my arms around myself, pulling my head down. I felt wretchedly guilty. "I don't want to be used as a trophy."

"Then what are you doing here? Come on! You set this up yourself. Why was it okay when I lost, but not him?"

"He's like my little brother."

"He wouldn't like to hear you say that."

"I know," I wailed. "I know."

Some time during the day's events, Dan's resolve had set. What had been a possibility, an idea, was now a clear intention. At dinner he set about gathering support. Shrewdly, he started with Louise.

"I upset your son today."

"I know." She had been well-disposed towards him at the start, because of the guests he had sent her. Her face was grim now.

"I'm sorry. I should have spoken to you first. We won't let this impact your business. If anything, it will improve things. I'm thinking we could work together, offer a variety of experiences, differentiate ourselves and give people choices. But share facilities: we'll have sporting facilities, a spa, gym, etc. Your guests could have access to those, and we could maybe even share a booking system. I'm determined to make it work for you. If this is going to fly we need the support of the town, and that means starting with you."

I could see her begin to thaw, but you would have to know her well to realise. "So what was that all about with Jason? I've hardly ever seen him so angry."

Dan put on a three-year-old's pout, put his hands in his pocket, shuffled his feet. "He beat me at tennis." He turned his face on edge and gave her a half smile. "I behaved badly. Forgive me?"

Like the boy who wants to get caught with his hand in the cookie jar, just to practise the art of eliciting forgiveness. How could you trust a man like that? I didn't expect Louise to fall for it, but she did. Cuffing him lightly across the head, she frowned once more and then laughed. "Be nice. Apologise to him."

We turned in unison to where she pointed. Jason had slunk in the back door while they had been talking.

Dan sauntered over, put out his hand. Over the babble of half a dozen conversations between us I couldn't hear what he said but I saw Jason's expression relax, the corners of his mouth twitch and he took Dan's hand. The man was a marvel. How did he manage to charm everyone? Couldn't they see through him? Surely I wasn't as weak as everyone else. Heaven help me if I was.

42

Somehow, over the course of the evening, Dan's plan became accepted, a fact. His conversations twisted from the theoretical to the practical with imperceptible verbal sleight of hand. While I was still trying to analyse how he did it, he had everyone present on board. They began talking timescales and strategy. I wanted to yell for everyone to stop. This wasn't how I'd planned things. This wasn't my vision. It was too soon to accept such a big change. I followed after him, trying to reverse things, add a note of caution, but it was too late, they all looked at me as if I were mad.

"But don't you see? This will change everything." My voice was louder now, loud enough for the room to go quiet in response.

"Maybe change it for the better," Peter called out, gently taunting.

I looked around. Dad had come to the kitchen door and was wiping his hands on his apron. His expression was cynically amused, like when he had watched my childish, righteous tantrums.

"We need to stop. Think about this. Think about what we want."

"Could it be," Peter continued, eyes twinkling, "that you don't like this idea because you didn't think of it yourself?"

Everyone watched me. Some were quietly laughing. I had to lock my knee to stop myself stamping my foot. I was a seven-year-old again, determined to convince them I was right. One of the old guys punched Dan encouragingly on the shoulder, a show of solidarity. He winked. "She's a feisty one, isn't she, our Jo? One of a kind." The most maddening thing was that in their humour they were still proud of me. I felt like an indulged, pretty, underestimated child.

Weak, too. When it came time to leave and he turned the full force of his smile on me I was so tempted to just go with him. I pulled against the hand that held mine. "Oh, come on, Jo. Don't be a sore loser."

"That's not it. I'm serious. This needs more thinking about."

"Why don't you let them make their own decisions? And anyway, who better to do that thinking than you and me? Come with me, we'll go back to the pod and think."

I could tell by his face that he didn't mean it. He was teasing me, trying to coerce me back to his bed. God, I so wanted to go.

We were walking back home with Dad and Grandad, and to give myself space to think I lagged back until I was walking between them. "She's angry at me," Dan said to Grandad. "You'll talk to me, though, if she won't?"

Grandad glanced at me and I nodded. He and Dan stepped ahead and I hung back, walking slower, so that Dad and I fell further behind.

"You okay?"

"Yeah."

"Had a bit of a rough time."

"Yeah. Didn't see you rushing to defend me." I was annoyed with myself for being sullen. Surely by now I should have grown out of taking things out on my dad.

He just laughed. "Defend you? Do you remember the last time I tried that? Told some kid to stop picking on you. You bit me, and told me to keep out of it and wouldn't talk to me all day. You said I had insulted your pride."

I remembered the incident clearly. I felt my face go hot.

"So, what is it? Do you really think this is a bad idea?"

"No, but I don't know. It's too fast. Dan's so ... charming, engaging ... convincing. But when you look back on what he's said, there's no substance to it."

"You don't trust him?"

I stopped walking, considering this. "That's it. I don't trust him."

Dad had stopped, too, and turned to face me. "Well, neither do I. But that doesn't mean he's wrong."

I stared into Dad's eyes, looking for an answer. "I just feel like I don't know him. I don't understand him."

"But you love him?"

"Yes. I think I do. Is that crazy? It's crazy, isn't it?"

"I didn't understand your mother, totally, either. And I know Grandad didn't understand very much of what your grandmother said at all."

"But he did understand her. Just in a different way."

"We're not going to be able to stop this. If he wants to do his development, it will happen. Everyone wants it. They're excited by the work, and the money coming into the community. You liked the place he did in Queenstown."

"Yes."

"So why would this be any less okay?"

I turned this over in my mind.

"Maybe what you need to consider is not . . . now, don't get mad . . . is not how to run the town, but how to manage your heart. I don't want to see you hurt, it would break my heart."

"You? You've been such a grumpy old bugger lately, I'd forgotten you had one."

"I just worry for you, when you go at things so hard."

"But, Dad, that's who I am. I always have done. It's time to get used to it. Things always work out all right. Well? Haven't they?"

"I suppose so. Yes. But it's never been about a guy before. We've never tried that one out."

"That's true. That's true." I had a thought – this was all about transferable skills. If I failed at something, I dusted myself off and tried something else. No problem. If I could do it with the rest of life, I could do it with love. I smiled. Dad smiled back, hesitantly. "Well, that's okay then. I'm glad we got that sorted out."

I skipped ahead, turning in at our gate. What was there to lose, after all?

43

Dan left the next morning to go back to his office, sort through some figures and send through a more detailed plan to his bosses. He left Dad and Peter in charge of widening the support and he wanted me to put together a CV so he could put me on the payroll with an official job title. I was nervous, but maybe Peter was right. I'd got so used to having everything in my control. A salary would be nice - it would be great to be contributing financially to the household. I decided to take a step back, and see how things unfolded as the detailed plans became clear.

As an added bonus, Dan sent more guests, both to Louise and to us. He had insisted on paying in full for the time he'd spent, and now the income from the pod looked set to continue. Dad didn't say much but I could see the relief on his face. He was doing hardly any arborist work now - there wasn't much work around, and he was busy with the restaurant anyway. People paid what they could afford for the food, but sometimes that barely covered the ingredients. Hardly any money had been coming in for a while.

"Do you think we should set a minimum price for dinner?"

"No. We don't want to lose the locals. It's still partly a charity, you said so yourself. For those sad no-hopers."

"I wasn't so rude. But can you keep going?"

"You know the plan. Once we have more tourists paying the flat $40 it'll be easy. We always knew that would take time to build up."

I took advantage of the lull in activity to phone Leonie at the university, let her know what was happening, get her perspective.

"For now, I'm just going with it. I'm the only one with reservations, it seems. At the moment it's so vague I can't argue against it. And who knows, maybe once I see it all laid out, I won't want to."

"It's mainly the size of it that concerns you?"

"And the outside money. If the investment is outside the town, the profit will go that way too."

"But they'll spend in town, where they can? Source food and workers and supplies?"

"So they say. I'm not sure you can guarantee it, though. What if they find a better price elsewhere?"

"Well, you know the old saying, Business is Business. But I've got an idea."

"What?"

"You could suggest they play up their community commitment on their web-site. It's a good idea for them, people love corporate responsibility. That's their intention, after all. If they put it in writing, in public, it will be easier for them to rationalise sticking to it."

"Brilliant! God, it's such a relief to talk to you! Someone who sees things clearly but isn't involved."

"No sweat. Did you have any more ideas about enrolling formally for a Master's, or a Ph.D?"

"Not yet. My head is still spinning. I'm keeping records, logging progress. I have continuing case studies on ten of the families and businesses in town, where they started, how they're doing. I don't have a clear picture yet of where it's going. Plus I might take that job Dan is offering, if the hotel complex goes ahead."

"You know if you were enrolled there's much more help I can give you. Maybe even get you funding to go see some of these other Slow Towns."

"I think it's best to let this evolve on its own, not try to fit it to some pattern. Thanks, though. I appreciate . . . well, everything."

"Sure. Call me if you need anything else."

I hung up and wandered into the kitchen. It was clean, empty-feeling. Dad had taken all of his favourite equipment down to Louise's. I looked at the clock. Two. For the first time in weeks I had nothing to do. I found a novel amongst the detritus on the coffee table and threw myself on the couch to read. It felt so good to lose myself for a few hours, forget everything. Life had begun to look so serious. I'd certainly been taking myself way too seriously.

Half way through the next morning, Dan called.

"Hey. How's it going?" I felt my cheeks stretch in a smile.

"Great. I'm having fun. My desk is covered with paper, and I've been on the phone to the States for over an hour, kicking around more Slow Time ideas. The more we can build in from the start, the better."

I told him about Leonie's idea, the community page on the web-site – without mentioning the original rationale, of course.

"Great idea. I'll keep that in the back of my mind. Can you get James to send the list of businesses he's working with for the Slow application? That will make a great reference for local resources."

"Sure. I'll ask him."

"So, I called to ask you a favour. Are you doing anything the next couple of days?"

"Nothing important."

"Would you bring your grandad down?"

"Grandad? Why?"

"I was telling the investors about him, about his perspective on life. I've kind of been trying to think through his eyes and brain a bit while I've been planning. I want this place to be unique and he has that alternative thought process thing going on. But, of course, I'm not as good at being him as he is."

"And you want him to come to you there?"

"I think it would work best. He's a little quiet with his friends and family around. We'll pay him. And you, if you can bring him."

"Okay. I'll ask him. Actually I think he'll be chuffed. I'll let you know."

44

Grandad and I set off the next morning. He had dusted off his old suit and tie and sat in the passenger seat with his hands bunched on his knees, trying to keep the fabric from creasing. I glanced over as we hit the open road sign on the outskirts of town.

"You good?"

"Yeah, fine." He smiled a small, secret smile, then frowned. "You don't think he'll ask me anything too hard?"

"He won't ask you anything you can't answer. He wants your opinion, that's all, and your ideas."

He shook his head in disbelief. Grandad wasn't used to people soliciting his opinion. "And he's going to pay me for that?"

"Yup. So you must be worth it."

"I don't know about that." The smile was back.

"Are you going to get big-headed?"

He lifted his chin, his eyelids lowering. "You mind your tongue, young lady."

"So that's a yes, then?"

"Well, maybe it is." We both laughed.

"Want to put on some music? Have a look in the glove box."

He chose Kelly Clarkson and inclined his ear intently to the songs as they played once through. On the second playing he found a track he liked and we heard it over and over and over again.

"Think we might have had enough of that one, Grandad?" I asked as he pushed the skip backwards button for the eleventh time.

"I like to really hear it. Do you mind, Jo? I won't do it if you mind."

I could have bitten my tongue. He was so sensitive. "No, Grandad, I don't mind. If you want to hear it again, we will."

Dan showed us around again before we sat down to talk. Things had changed since I had been there in December. The kitchen was busy and the restaurant was well occupied for lunch. There were only a few empty rooms. We walked down to the lake and back, then Dan asked Grandad where he'd like to look at the plans.

He turned to me, unsure. "I like the view of the lake. It'll help us think."

"The restaurant, then? It will quieten down soon."

"Yes. The restaurant. Near the window."

"Great. I'll just go and get my papers."

Grandad sat and looked out at the view. He seemed unaware of me and I watched him without speaking. I sensed he was going through some deeply personal preparation ritual and I realised I had witnessed this process in him many times before. But before what? What did it mean?

Dan returned. Grandad looked down at the papers.

"We don't need your pictures yet. Put them away. We're going to talk about this thing you call Slow."

Dan put his notes aside on the next table, moving calmly. "What do you call it?"

"I call it Life."

Dan nodded. I felt myself compelled to stay back, observe without participating.

"I've been watching what happens when people start to move Slow. They start to understand things – I never realised they didn't understand before."

"What things do they start to understand?"

I wanted to kick Dan, but he was out of reach. Just let him talk, let him take his time.

Grandad's forehead creased with the effort of bringing his thoughts around to answer the question.

"It's okay, Grandad. You just talk. Dan's questions will get answered in their own time."

Dan turned to me, curious. I gave him a mock-ferocious glare. He nodded, and I saw his body relax further into his chair. "I'm sorry, yes, just go on. You never realised they didn't understand . . ."

There was a long pause. I felt the mood of preparation again. Dan and I watched Grandad watching the almost motionless view. I felt an alteration and didn't know if it was in the room or in me.

"Some of them don't like it when things begin to come clear. Those are the ones who go back to their nervous ways." Again his forehead creased. "I don't know whether it's just not their time, or if that will be life for them always. Others, the first thing they think is they want to help people. You need to build that into your hotel."

Dan turned towards his papers again. I shook my head and he subsided, then in a moment was leaning forward in his chair.

"Then the next thing, they start to remember their dreams. People's dreams separate them. They are unique, like the pieces of a jigsaw puzzle. That's how the world is supposed to be, with everybody taking their place and fitting together. People move into that when they start to go Slow. So you need to build that into your hotel as well."

I felt Dan's impatience. He wasn't disagreeing, but he didn't understand. Wait. Just wait. I saw him open his mouth to speak again and went to sit beside him, placing my hand on his arm. I was impatient, too, but if we tried to hurry this we would lose it altogether. Grandad glanced at me and I smiled. Dan put his hand on mine and left it there. We held our breath.

"The shape of people changes," Grandad went on. "Sometimes it's just for a time and sometimes it's forever. Your dad, Jo, he has his new shape more and more. He's losing that . . ." He searched for a word and didn't find one, making a jittery gesture with his hand instead. I knew exactly what he meant. I knew the mood personally, too, I had inherited it from Dad. I wanted to ask if I was losing it too, but again held back. Wait. Listen.

"There are some things that people need to know as they start to become Slow. They need to know that helping can be an . . . upward thing. They seem to look for things wrong to fix – sick people or desperate people. But you can help people who are already happy. You can contribute to things that are already good."

"Like what?" I bit my tongue, chastised myself for interrupting.

"Like . . . helping someone who has things they need to learn before they can do what they need to do."

"Like a scholarship?"

"Maybe."

Dan pinched me and I gave him a tiny nod of acknowledgement.

"Okay. Go on. We're listening."

"Then they need space to work out the details of their own puzzle piece. I've noticed they are very hazy. They talk . . . like they've borrowed a voice. It takes time before they . . . find . . ." He tailed off, staring out the window again. I let my breath out and allowed my thoughts to follow his half sentence out into the view. It takes time before they find their own voice, their own detail, the individuality of their dream. People talk in broad words: "artist", "writer", "helping people", as if those were cookie cutters to shape the breadth of life. The detail was missing, the uniqueness. I felt Grandad's attention return to the room. He straightened up, spoke faster. "So you need to build that into your hotel as well. That's all."

"That's all?" Dan said. He looked bewildered.

"That's all. You write that down. I'm going for a walk."

Dan watched him out of the room with his mouth hanging open. "Did you get all that?"

I laughed. "I think so. It wasn't what you expected?"

"How could I have expected that?"

"Well, you asked for it."

"How in hell do we translate that into . . . anything? Anything concrete?"

"Just relax. I have a feeling it will be easy, it will be obvious once we just let it sit for a while, talk it around. He's right, if you're going to provide for people making a change in their lives, you have to understand the change and how it's happening."

"And how do we do that without having that change happen to us?"

I pulled back in surprise. "Well, we don't! We have to let the change happen. Otherwise what is the point?"

"But I like the way I am. I don't want to change."

"Then what is the point?"

"I don't know. I really don't. I had it so clear, and now I have no idea."

"I think maybe we should go for a walk, too, then, and let it come back again."

Grandad's words were echoing in my mind. I trusted them even though I couldn't immediately connect them up with what I already knew. Here and there they hooked on. Perhaps he was nudging at me a little bit with his comment about helping people without fixing them. I liked the idea of a totally unique life, too, a totally unique contribution. This resonated deep within me. But then how did that translate to a physical building, or set of buildings, or even a wider environment? Dan was talking to one of the local farmers about buying some land, 40 hectares that spread across a beautiful valley backed in the distance by permanently snow-capped mountains. Even in that context, how did this apply? We would bring the view in for contemplation, as he had here, of course. But that in itself was nothing like enough.

Dan wanted to talk and talk, spinning Grandad's words into an endless running circle.

"Slow down. We'll work it out. This is a whole new thing."

"But it's so exasperating! He has something special and he can't communicate it! God, was this a waste of time?"

I pulled Dan around to face me, briefly revelling in the sense of my superior power, better control. "Relax. He has communicated everything he needs to. It just takes a new perspective. Allow yourself to make the shift. Trust the process of your mind. Let his ideas find their own place amidst the practical details you're so good at."

"But I always start with vision before the details make sense. I'm blind here. I hate it."

"Give it time. We want a hotel that encapsulates Slow, right?"

"Yes, I know that!"

"And we had some ideas already: artists' studio, individual spaces, beauty in surroundings."

"Yes. Yes! Obvious. I wanted more. I wanted him to take us the next step."

"And I think he has. He's shown us."

"How?"

"Calm! You won't have insight in this mood. And you can't use logic. And you can't expect him to describe it with precision like it was a shopping list. Let your mind go. Let your thoughts float with those two ideas: the physical hotel, and his vision."

I felt Dan's mood subside a little. "And what is that, precisely? I've lost track."

I thought for a moment, to sum it up. "Help people express the uniqueness of their dreams and contribution."

Dan repeated it.

"Yes."

"And wait for insight."

"Yes."

"That's very Zen. Okay. I think I can do that." We walked on further until we found a seat by the lake. A pair of herons swooped over the water, a good luck omen, and all was still.

45

The technique that made me so successful academically was to trust the workings of my unconscious. While other people were panicking and rushing, I took in the terms of an assessment immediately we were given it and let it sit, completely untended, until I had the impulse to do it now. Sometimes that was weeks before it was required, sometimes it was very last minute, but I trusted the process and it always worked.

Dan liked to be in conscious control of the tasks in front of him. That had always worked for him before, but now he was in uncharted territory with an oracle as a guide and no previous experience to help him. In contrast I felt a deep, floating trust that everything would work out well. It felt like home. I realised I had forgotten this process, had not thought to transfer it to what we were doing in the town. I felt blissful freedom and release. This exasperated Dan.

"Will you stop looking so smug!"

"No. I feel great. You're not going to stop me."

"Well, give me what you've got then. I want to feel like you do.'

"I've already given it to you. You just didn't pick it up."

"Do you know how annoying you are?"

"Yes. But beautiful and charming, too. Why don't you concentrate on that for a while?"

"Because I'm working on the hotel. Which you should be, too, since I'm paying you."

"You can't work on it by working on it. I told you. Relax! The answer will come."

"That's exactly what I plan to tell my bosses in my report. Item: consultation with a sprite and her ancestor. Result: nothing. But don't worry, the answer will come."

My delighted laughter surprised me. I felt like I'd just come out of my final exam, like a pressure that had built imperceptibly over weeks and months had been removed in a moment. I was euphoric, and I found his frustration irresistible. "Trust. Trust me, trust Grandad, trust yourself. It will work out." I stepped in front of him, turned my face up to his, reached up to kiss him. He turned away. "Here, come with me. Show me your room."

He turned back, looking into my face again, head tilted, tempted. Then he shook his head. "I have to work."

"This is work. It's essential you be distracted. Let your mind go."

"Will you stop saying that!"

I took his hand, and after a further brief show of reluctance he pulled me to him, kissed me, turned towards reception.

"Katie, when the old man comes back, will you show him to the lake cabin – I think it's 14 that's free, no? Tell him I'm in a meeting. I'll come and find him when I'm done."

We walked along the ground floor corridor to a private staircase at the far end. It wound up two flights of narrow spiral to a wide room with the best view so far, a wall of uninterrupted glass. There were sofas, a desk and, screened off at one end, on a raised platform, a large bed with dark, heavy linen sheets.

"Shall I draw us a bath? It might help me relax." His impish smile was back, his focus entirely on me again.

"Sure." As he left the room I reflected that I liked it better when he was off-balance. I preferred him a little unsure. Maybe that was what people meant when they said to keep someone guessing, keep a little mystery. It had never made sense before. Caroline was happy with Mikey, and she was totally transparent. But Mikey wasn't Dan. I preferred things more exciting. Dan had said life was a game, and I had thought that sounded selfish. But now I'd had a taste of the other side, the upper hand, I realised I liked it. Maybe I could play this game after all.

At dinner Dan was excited, manic. The distraction had worked and he was having idea after idea after idea, talking and sketching and making notes, asking Grandad questions and guiding him through to an answer that satisfied.

I was still catching my breath from the exhilaration of the afternoon. I hadn't thought myself passive before, but taking the game into the equation had transformed the experience. Dan was high and I was mellow, floating. I didn't care about anything, I didn't hear half of what was said. It was like watching television with the sound off.

Dan occasionally slid a piece of paper towards me, asked for my approval. I just smiled and nodded, my head full of air. Maybe this was what it felt like to be a bimbo. I'd always thought they lacked brains, but perhaps it was just that after hours of fabulous sex they didn't care to use them. I laughed, a tinkling, vacuous, airhead laugh. Whatever. Who cares?

My dreams were vivid and arousing. When I woke in the morning I had the impression I had reached for Dan more than once during the night. His expression was extremely self-satisfied, so probably I had. There was something new in him, also. He was changed. Bigger. More confident. I wouldn't have thought it possible.

As the morning progressed my thoughts slowly returned towards normal. Grandad was out walking again, this time with a couple he had met at breakfast. Dan wanted to go through the plans without him; the detail confused him, we were better to frame specific questions especially for him rather than include him at this stage.

The phone rang. Dan leaned back to pick it up and I took his place at the desk, flipping through the copious notes we had made. It was exciting, the way it was taking shape, not so far from standard but with subtle, fundamental differences.

I heard the tone of Dan's voice change and looked up. He was looking at me. "Yes, that's right. It's a good price for the area. You've seen the pictures? . . . Yes, it's farmland. It's a dairy area, so the price per hectare reflects that . . . The plan is to make it a destination . . . Yes, I'm sure it can work . . . I know, it's entirely new, there are other places in the world with this general focus, but not . . . Yes, an experiment, but it's so clear, it's guaranteed . . ." His brow furrowed. I felt his body tense, the change invisible. "I'm absolutely sure . . . Yes . . . Yes . . . Yes . . . I will . . . I'll ask her. We'll talk again tomorrow."

I realised my mouth was open and dry. I felt very nervous. "What?"

Dan took in my expression and burst out laughing. "You look so worried!"

"Well, it sounded like they're having second thoughts. They're not sure."

"Yes, that's true."

"So they might not do it? We might not be able to do it?"

He rolled his chair back towards mine and wrapped his arms around my waist. "Remember, life's a game, now it's our play. I sent them some notes this morning, it's new for them, like it was for me. They need us to sell it to them. That was always true. You've always got to convince the money. It's part of the game."

"Us? They need us to sell it to them?"

"Sure. They want to see us in the States, as soon as makes sense. We'll go next week, once the plans are further along."

"So it's not certain? It might not happen?" I felt the bottom fall out of my stomach, like part of me was telescoping away.

"Of course it will happen. And yes, at the moment it's uncertain. But we'll convince them. I told you. It's part of the game."

"I don't like this game any more."

"You want certainty?"

"Yes, please."

He laughed again. "Let your mind go, Sweetheart! It's certain that life is uncertain. Once you get over that, everything is fine."

Grandad wanted to go home. He said he had things he needed to do, but I knew he'd just reached his limit and he was homesick. We packed up the car and Dan stood making his farewell. Grandad was staring at the cheque in his hand. "$4,000. This can't be right."

"Eight hours' consulting, $500 per hour. Standard rate."

I had a similar cheque in my pocket, and had had a similar reaction, but I'd tried to hide it.

"It doesn't make sense." Grandad shook his head and looked up at Dan, head tilted.

Dan just nodded, knowing how to reassure him. He put a hand on his arm. "I appreciate your help, your vision. It's been a gift without price." He opened the car door and gestured Grandad inside, closing it gently. I met him at the back of the car and pressed myself into his embrace. This parting felt unbearable. A new kind of love. I took strength from him silently, then twisted out of his grip. He groped the air after me. I forced a playful smile. I'd have to practise my impression of nonchalance.

"See ya," I said, slipping into my seat and pulling away, as fast as was decent, tearing my eyes from his parting wave and back towards the road.

46

Before I met Dan I would have been nervous about meeting billionaires the same way I would be nervous about meeting a prime minister, or a famous artist. With the distinctions Dan had drawn I now expected a different species, an alien life form.

The car that picked us up from the airport was nice, understated. It was weird having a chauffeur but not fundamentally different from being in a taxi, despite his tailored suit and quiet discretion. The house we pulled up in front of was similar to a pleasant country hotel. It wasn't until we were inside, and being greeted by the owners, that the world shifted, the air took on a different taste. These people were not remotely like anyone else I'd ever met before.

Charm, politeness, kind concern over jetlag, the accented English, these were pleasant but nothing new; what stunned me was the unearthly good health of both husband and wife. They glowed with an inner power. I tried to put my finger on it, but didn't know where to begin.

"Excuse me," I blurted out, "but do all billionaires look like you?"

They turned to each other and laughed. "No," said the woman. "Some of them have heart attacks before they're fifty. I'm Alice." She shook my hand.

"And I'm John." Alice and John. Perfectly human. Just radiating a glow like Raphael's angels.

"I'm Jo. Joanna. Jo. God, excuse me, I'm nervous and jetlagged and ..."

"Stopping talking right now," said Dan, turning to our hosts. "Didn't I tell you she was gorgeous?"

"You did. You also told us other people talk the way you do, and we didn't believe you."

I turned to Dan, uncertain. "They're making fun of your accent. Don't worry, they've been to New Zealand many times; they know it's normal."

"Not making fun. Never making fun. It's like being back there, just hearing you. Like a holiday. We love it."

I don't know what I had expected. Straight down to business, maybe, moved on and out of the way so they could get on with their busy and important lives.

In contrast they seemed to have all the time in the world for us. Alice was a master of fascinated listening; I felt interesting, witty, brilliant, the whole time her face was fixed on mine. She interjected personal details that made me feel like I knew her too. I was enchanted.

John was a comedian, with finely observed commentary on life and the world delivered in a warm, dry manner; nothing less would have distracted me from my conversation with Alice.

We had drinks by the pool. They chatted briefly with Dan about the Queenstown hotel; they trusted him, he had their confidence, it seemed more like idle interest than an investors' enquiry.

In the afternoon we went horse riding, something I hadn't done since my mother died and Dad couldn't face seeing her horses day after day. I still remembered. I had ridden every day from four to seven. Alice's face was a picture of concern when I told her about it. It embarrassed me.

"I wasn't looking for sympathy, I just . . ."

"I know you weren't, Darling. I know."

I wanted to know the details of their lives, what they spent their time on. It couldn't all be drinks and outdoor pursuits. We must be interrupting something important. But I didn't know how to ask.

"You must have lots of projects you're involved in," I hinted.

Alice smiled. "You think making money should look different from this?"

"Well, yes. I expected . . . I don't know, I don't want to be rude."

She nodded encouragingly.

"I expected a house full of servants and meetings in skyscrapers and, I don't know, lots of rush."

"Sometimes the better you manage things the less you have to do. We prefer to work with a few people who are passionate about what they do. Like Dan. People who have a lot to contribute, and the energy to make something happen, and they just need finance. Pick the right person, a few phone calls, a few discussions, and let them go."

"But this is pretty small for you?"

"We have bigger projects, yes. But that's not really how I judge things. I love this new idea you have. I liked the eco aspect of Dan's last project, but this one has more heart, somehow."

"It does. It's my family, my town. My life, actually."

Alice bit her lip. I sensed there was something she wasn't saying.

"What?"

"Nothing, Honey. You'll work it out."

"Work what out? Please?"

"Well, it's your family, and your town. And maybe your life, for now. But not for long. I don't think it will be your life for long. They'll get on their feet and you'll move on."

I began to protest. It sounded so callous.

"I mean it as a compliment. You're bigger than this one small town. It will always be home, but a home to come back to. You'll leave, but you'll make a success of this first. Everyone will be fine."

The conversation we came all this way to have was so subtle I missed it. I blinked, and then Dan was shaking hands with both of them and we were heading home.

"What happened?'

"They liked you."

"And that's it? That was all there was to it?"

"Yup. That's all."

"I don't believe it!"

Dan laughed. I stared out the window at the passing countryside. "You mean I meet their standards? I'm one of their trusted people?"

"Yup."

"Wow!" and my face broke into the broadest, brightest smile.

47

As the project progressed, I thought a lot about what Alice had said. Pick the right person and trust them. The better you manage things the less you have to do. She'd suggested I try meditating, as a way to centre myself and keep everything on track. I didn't have the patience for it, sitting still in a quiet room and thinking about nothing. I felt like a failure until someone suggested it might be easier to let the mind float free if I went out walking.

I asked around and found one of the people at the retirement village had a dog - a little Westie - which she couldn't get out to walk as much as she liked. Every morning just before dawn I arrived at her back door, took the lead from the hook in the porch and unlocked the cat door from the outside so he could come out. If the lights were on I'd knock, say good morning, and then we were off, my eyes following his delighted little body as he sniffed and shook and turned, letting my mind float as Alice suggested, noticing my thoughts then letting them go.

I experienced occasional blinding flashes of insight, more frequent wild, excellent and random ideas, answers to things I'd been puzzling over. More profound, and not obviously related, was the calm that settled over me at other times of the day. I saw more clearly, found decisions easier, was now able to focus on the people involved in the processes rather than just the processes themselves.

As the building got under way, Dan moved to town. He wanted to come with me on these walks but I said no. This was my time.

Things started accelerating quickly. James was in the final stages of the Slow City application with the delegation visit in a few days. Dan was working with our young web designers to improve the web-site. He brought in a professional designer, tactfully having her work with the kids, teach them at the same time as making the refinements necessary to complete a great site and have it rate well in the search engines. She found relevant blogs for me to comment on, linking back to our site.

"It's way more effective than starting your own blog. You get synergy with other people's efforts. They'll be excited about what's happening here, too, and flattered that you've noticed them. It's win-win."

I was filled with awe, watching the building take shape. The vague image I had from looking at the plans was replaced in leaping stages, first the foundations, which looked way too small for anything like the number of rooms and guests. Then the framing, making no more sense to me than a house of cards as it went up. We walked around inside, Dan pointing around and talking as if he already saw solid walls and lit fireplaces. I held my tongue and waited, knowing it would become clearer in time.

The Italian delegation came. James seemed to grow in stature with the respect they gave him as of right as mayor – in Folkstown he was just plain old James Smith, like he had always been, despite the relatively new title. That's the way people are around here. But the Italians treated him like royalty, and he loved it.

Dad was in his element, showing off his restaurant, and Dan was at his most urbane as he took them through the hotel site, speaking in understated tones about his ideas and intentions, frighteningly impressive.

I stayed in the background, feeling totally out of place. Louise chided me. "Get in there, take the credit, it's yours."

"I can't. I know, well, I sort of know, but I can't. As long as they like us, as long as they want us to be one of them, that's enough."

She frowned, but to my relief she didn't push it and a few days later they made their farewells, nodding and smiling. James was confident we would get their official approval soon.

We continued building pods in the town, more and more people joining this project as stories of success spread. Dad was earning enough from his to live on, meaning he could relax about the restaurant. Ironically as he did that, it started spinning money. The guests in the pods went there almost every night and, as they spent money in the town, the locals were contributing more, paying more for their dinners, too.

"You know I was never in it for the profit, Jo."

"I know, Dad. But people who do what they love with passion and commitment are supposed to be rewarded. That's how the world works. Enjoy it."

He grinned. "Well, it's easier being the cheerful host knowing that I'll be able to afford tomorrow's ingredients. I have thoughts of redecorating the house, too. What do you think?"

I felt a change in my body, a shifting from head to heart. Mum had chosen the wallpaper and the paint colours. Nothing had been done to it since then. "Well, maybe a new bathroom? But take it easy, there's no rush."

It didn't make sense for me to mind one way or the other. Dan had taken the flat above the souvenir shop – partly to help the owners, who had been struggling, until things picked up – and my regular visits were now formalised: I was living there, too. This new level of commitment and stability made me shiver, part pleasure and part disbelief. I told myself I was still taking things one day at a time.

48

It was mid-winter now, frosty as we stepped out of the restaurant. I was grateful we had only metres to walk home. Dan put his arm around me and pulled me close.

"That was a good night. Nancy gets funnier every day."

"I thought she looked a little frail tonight."

"It's just the cold. Your Grandad's looking after her."

"Yes. He's very kind."

"And besotted."

It was true. The softness in his eye as he watched Nancy had become clearer and stronger over time. I wondered if he knew what he was feeling.

"Honestly, I'd like to see the old one happy. Do you think they'd get together properly?"

I covered my surprise as I unlocked the door and started up the stairs to the flat. "I hadn't thought about it."

"I don't know if he has, either, but I think Nancy would be keen. Why don't you suggest it?"

I laughed. "Then I just need to get Dad set up and they'd be properly off my hands. Louise, do you think?"

"Why not? Then you and Jason could round off the inter-family set."

I turned away to hang up my scarf. "Are we back to that again? I wish you'd leave him alone."

"I don't like the way he looks at you. He could be dangerous."

"Don't be ridiculous. And don't pretend it's about me. You just love the fight."

"It's fun, I admit, especially because I win every day."

"Exactly. I'm here, so why taunt him?"

Dan shrugged. I could never get a satisfactory answer out of him about this.

"I wish he'd go," I sighed. "He'd have much better opportunities in Christchurch."

"You don't want him to leave. Be honest."

"Of course I do. I want what's best for him."

"No you don't! You like having a little acolyte around. And you half fancy him."

I could never tell if Dan was serious when he talked like this. He sounded like he believed it, but it was probably part of some side game he was playing. I didn't bother to contradict him. It would only make him dig in more.

"Anyway, he's wasted working for Minnie."

"The legendary Minnie. I wish I knew her more. But she won't talk to me, no matter how friendly I am."

"Ancient family feud. Don't interfere."

"But I think I should. I'm going to make it a project. Heal the rift."

"Forget it, Dan. Just leave it." I shouldn't let him get to me. This was just the sort of reaction he loved, and it brought out the worst in him. "I'm going to have a shower. Turn on my electric blanket for me?"

"I can keep you warm, Babe."

I hate it when he calls me that.

SLOW TIME

49

Grandad and I stood together as a film crew set up in the restaurant. They were making a news clip about the town and somehow the story had shifted from the Slow concept to Nancy-the-70-year-old-standup. Dan said not to worry, there would be plenty of opportunities to get the town on the news once our Slow City status came through.

Nancy was grinning at the camera, jiggling like an excited four-year-old.

"She's great, isn't she?"

"She is, Grandad." I paused, choosing my words. "Have you thought about asking her out?"

His head pulled back and he turned to look at me. "On a date, you mean?"

"Yes. I notice you like her."

"Everyone likes her. She's beautiful."

"Yes. But I think she's even more special to you."

He turned back to her, the softness immediately in his eye again. "I think you're right." He nodded. "I'll ask her. Just to see. Thanks, Jo."

"Any time."

Three days later we wheeled a television in so we could watch the news as we ate. A cheer went up as Nancy came on the screen, followed by lots of shushing. It was amazing. She was even funnier than in person, either because she was playing up for the camera, or just because it was so surprising to see her there.

"You could have a career at this," someone shouted.

"I think I already have," Nancy replied, and emptied a bowl of chips so she could pass it round, pretending to ask for money.

It was time for me to do the next round of questionnaires for the ten families I was following for my research. I still had no idea when or if I would write it up, but it felt right to keep going with what I had started, especially when the news almost everywhere was good.

Now that things had picked up so far it was hard to remember the pain and uncertainty of the beginning. That worst moment, when I had to close Louise's café down, seemed so unreal now that the place rang with laughter and life every night.

I stepped into slow motion as I walked into each living room, looked into each well-fed and happy face. The questions that had been painful eight, nine, ten months ago were joyful now. I felt a warm glow to think it was partly thanks to me.

"Entirely thanks to you, Jo, not partly."

"No, Peter, no. Everyone's worked so hard."

"But without your vision, your guts . . ."

"You gave me credit, so we could do up the bed and breakfast. Without that . . ."

"Okay, Jo, okay, I give up. It's been a team effort. But now, isn't it time you did something for you?"

"What do you mean? This is for me. As much as for anyone."

Peter shook his head. "You had left here. Moved away. You came back, stayed back, to help us. Things will be fine now, the momentum is there. If you want to go there's no reason for you to stay."

"But I'm learning so much, with the hotel."

"That's good. That's enough for you at the moment?"

"And then there's Dan."

Peter looked doubtful.

"And there's following this study through . . ." I rushed on, then tailed off.

"Which you could do from a distance, if there was somewhere else you wanted to be."

I was unaccountably upset. "Are you saying I should go? People don't want me here?" I sat down and began to cry, not lightly; deep racking sobs. When I could look up I saw Peter, wide-eyed and horrified.

"That's not what I meant, Jo. Of course not."

"But you don't like Dan."

Peter pressed his lips together. "It's just that none of us wants to hold you back. You're so brilliant. You should follow your own path."

"I am. I will."

Peter's words echoed round and round in my head. From one direction or another I had heard a similar message many times; Peter was just more clear and more definite. Mixed up in it was the feeling that Dan wasn't good for me, but they didn't know, they didn't understand about the balance of our relationship, about how much it was teaching me about myself.

I dwelt on all this the next few mornings, following Archie on his snuffling daily walk. He still managed to find small piles of leaves to poke his nose into and I smiled as he came up shaking again and again.

This was what Alice had said, and Grandad, even Dan. You have to find the thing that is uniquely you and do it. My thoughts turned and turned, from thinking this was it, what I was doing here, to feeling that there was something more, somewhere, that I was still growing into my dreams.

I was learning, I knew that. Everything Dan was teaching me about the practicalities and considerations of getting a real business off the ground would be hugely valuable whatever I chose to do next. But was that just an excuse for delay, for staying where I was comfortable, where my bed was warm?

I turned my thoughts from this vexing question to an easier, more tangible concern: we already had forward bookings for the projected opening in October, and it made me nervous. What if we weren't ready? Dan had laughed when I said this. "It'll be okay. You'll see."

50

It was official! We had Slow City status, with a certificate, even a flag, and the film crew was returning to film the party. Finally we would have news that focused on the core of the town, our Slow City. That would bring tourists, surely, more and more people coming to stay, and talking about us. That would guarantee success.

I was still dressing for the party when the call came through from Alice. I put my hand over the receiver and whispered to Dan. "You go on, I need to take this."

I heard the door close behind him. "Hi Alice. You're up early. How are you? What is it?"

"I was just thinking of you, and I had a gut instinct to call. I know things are getting near to finished over there."

"Or near to started, depending how you look at it."

"The hotel will open in a month."

"That's right. It's going to be great."

"I've seen the pictures. It looks beautiful. But I called to talk about you."

"Me?"

"I think it's time you started thinking about what your next project will be."

"Funny. Everyone seems to be saying that lately."

"Well, there you are. One person could have their wires crossed, but when you start getting a message from more than one source, it's time to listen. Do you have any thoughts?"

"Well, my lecturer wants me to come back, do a post-graduate degree. Master's, or Ph.D."

"And what about you? What do you want?" I was silent. "Anyway, that's all I wanted to say. Think about it. I'd like to help, be part of it, whatever it is. Just let me know."

"Okay. Thanks. That's amazing. I can't believe it."

I heard her low, comforting laugh. "Believe it, Honey. The world is going to want to get on your bandwagon."

I wandered into the party in a daze, camera pointed into my expressionless face. I got past it as soon as I could and found Grandad holding hands with Nancy in a corner. I wanted the comfort of his presence, even if he didn't really have eyes for me just now.

I leaned back in my chair, watching. Dan was talking to the TV reporter, winking over at me, gesturing for me to join him. I stayed where I was. Dad and Louise were deep in conversation. I had meant my comment about the two of them to be a joke, but for the first time I thought there might be something in it. I caught Jason's eye and smiled. He hesitated for a moment, then walked over.

"Great party."

"Yeah. It got going fast!"

"Pretty exciting. This is what you've been working for, all this time."

"What?"

"The certificate, being a real Slow Town! What's up, Jo? You're not yourself."

"No. I'm not." I looked over at Grandad. He was whispering in Nancy's ear. No comfort here, then. "Can we go for a walk? I need to get out of the crowd."

SLOW TIME

51

We stepped into the cold air. "Just let me go back for a coat."

Jason followed me up the stairs, looking around him with intensity.

"You haven't been up here before."

"No."

"It's pretty basic."

"Yeah. I'd have thought Prince Charming would have wanted more luxury."

"It isn't to be had, really. But he's a simple guy, at heart."

"You don't expect me to believe that.'

"I'm not going to argue with you. Not tonight. Let's go." I grabbed my coat, scarf and gloves. I needed to be walking.

"So what about you, Jason? When are you going to leave, seek your fortune?"

"I'm happy here, for the moment."

"You were going to try out for the Crusaders. Why don't you do that?"

"I did. I didn't get in."

"Oh. I'm sorry. Why didn't you tell me?"

"Oh, like you go around touting your failures. But I forgot, you don't have any."

We walked on in silence for a minute or two.

"But really, Jason, what is the future here? Don't you want to be doing something more?"

"I'll leave when you do, Jo, how about that?"

I saw his point. It wasn't fair, me distracting myself from my uncertainty by attacking his.

"Thanks," I said, simply.

"For what?"

"For being here. For letting me talk. Life is so confusing."

"That's true. I've noticed that, too."

The news clip had its effect and we received an avalanche of enquiries. Hits on the web-site spiked over the next few days and we had about a hundred sign-ups for the newsletter. It was my job to write it and send it out. I drafted a few paragraphs and showed it to Dan. He had been cool since the party. My plan was to ignore it; I knew he'd get over himself eventually. He wasn't really jealous of Jason, it was just a pose.

"Sure. Fine."

"No 'well, done, Jo, brilliant!' "

"No. You don't deserve it."

"I don't or my work doesn't?"

"You. The writing's fine."

I stepped in front of him, putting my face close to his. "You don't love me any more."

"Not at the moment, no."

I kissed him. "Now."

"Nope."

I wrapped one leg around his waist, pressing myself against him, experiencing triumph as his body responded to mine. "Now."

"No. No, no, no."

"Yes you do. You can't fool me." I kissed him again, pushing him back onto his desk. Papers moved and slid to the floor. I pushed his arms out to the sides. He pretended to resist for a moment then relaxed, letting go. I felt something shift in my mind. I knew this moment, this scene, would be etched on my memory. We had made love so many times, why was this different? The answer echoed immediately from deep inside me. Love. He's in love. He's helpless. And at that moment I felt an exhilarating, dizzying sense of power.

SLOW TIME

52

Something new was happening. Our pod guests had often thanked me, said they had loved staying here, but now it was something more. They were claiming it had changed their lives.

It was true the town felt different. The official Slow Town status couldn't possibly have changed anything, could it? But I knew my steps were slower, when I was walking Archie, when I called in at the restaurant, when I went to the supermarket to buy supplies. Something was tangibly different, and everyone felt it. It was wonderful and unbelievable at the same time.

The hotel was open and Dan and I had moved into our suite, above the reception area, looking out towards the Southern Alps. I stepped out of bed each morning to stand at the picture window, feeling life was almost complete. Almost.

"Hey there. You're awake."

I turned and looked at Dan, leaning up on one elbow. "Good morning. Coffee?"

"Yes, please."

"You just wait here, I'll sneak down and get it."

I slipped into the bathroom and pulled jeans and t-shirt off the hook where I had left them last night. This would do for the few seconds I'd be downstairs. Later I'd dress up properly for the day, and my new professional persona. I was loving the role of hotel manager. I really felt like a grown-up.

The big Gaggia machine was already warmed up ready for the first breakfast sitting. I waved to the waitress, took hot cups from the top, heated the milk and swirled Dan's latte just the way he liked it. Mine was a short black, intense and brief, caffeine hitting some time after the last drop was gone.

I sat on the bed while he sipped, feeling a light and drifting peace. He smiled, his glowing morning smile, so beautiful. The morning light lit his face, making the skin more golden. I reached out and curled my hand around his cheek.

"I think it's time for me to leave." The words surprised me; I hadn't realised I was going to say them until they were out.

"Leave? What do you mean?"

"I'll stay a little longer, to get everything arranged. Then we can get someone else in. It doesn't need to be me."

"You're leaving me?"

"You were never going to stay here forever. You know that."

"But I thought . . . I thought we'd move on together. We're such a great team." He attempted his winning smile, but his face looked broken. "Where . . . where are you going to go?"

"I don't know yet. I need some time out, to think about that. Alice offered me her guest cottage for a week or so. I might go there. Or just travel. I've been stuck here for so long."

"Stuck here. I thought you loved it." He spoke, but the words were random, his mind was somewhere else. "Won't you . . . God, I don't even know what to say. This has never happened to me before."

I felt so strong, so callous. I looked at him as if he were ill.

"Don't you love me?" he pleaded.

"I thought I did. But I don't think so. Sorry." It was like I was someone else, some hard-hearted femme fatale in a movie. This wasn't nice, what I was doing, how I was doing it, but it felt right. It felt like what I was supposed to do.

My day was smooth, seamless. I talked to guests, arranged horse riding for them and called to town for more art supplies to be delivered. It was a crisp spring day and the air was clear. A group was going hiking, some with cameras. I took the hotel shuttle and delivered them to the start of the track, checking they all had food and wet weather gear, just in case.

At twelve I changed into my exercise clothes and went down to the gym. This was a new thing, something I had taken up once it wasn't practical to walk every day. I found myself working harder and harder on the treadmill. I got the personal trainer to show me how to use the weights. My body was shaping to my intention for the first time in my life. I was getting addicted to the sense of control.

This exercise was meditative, too, but in a different way from walking, more powerful, more intense. I was changing, and I liked it.

In the afternoon I called Dan in his office and asked him to take over for a couple of hours. "I want to go see Grandad."

Dan's voice was weak. "What are you going to tell him?"

"I don't know."

Grandad just looked at me, no expression in his eyes. "So you're doing it, too."

"Doing what?"

"Giving us up."

"No! What are you talking about? I've done all I can here."

He kept staring. "Nancy is leaving."

"How? Why?"

"They want her to do a tour. Shows around the country. She asked me to go."

"Nancy?" We'd have to find someone to fill the gap at the restaurant. She had become one of the major attractions. Busloads of people were coming to see her, filling the restaurant and the town. Dad was paying her, and she was making a heap in tips, too. "How long for?"

"Six weeks. They said it would be shorter, but at her age she needs more rest between shows."

"She'd do four shows a day without blinking. What do they mean?"

Grandad shrugged. He was different, somehow. Bitter. He was always accepting, always. This didn't suit him.

"You'll miss her."

His eyes filled. He nodded.

"So why don't you go, if she wants you to?"

"You know I get overwhelmed, Jo. Escalators. Lifts. So many people who don't know me. I couldn't do it. It's best not to try. And she'd be distracted. She wouldn't look at me. She doesn't need me."

I wanted to argue, but he was right. "She'll be back though."

"Yes."

"You'll wait for her."

"I suppose so."

"That's good then."

"Yes. But now you're going, too. You'll tear the life out of that boy. Dan. You'll hurt him."

"You said people need to follow their hearts, Grandad. I'm following my heart."

He looked directly at me, straight into my eyes. "You're following something. But it isn't your heart."

SLOW TIME

53

The criticism kept coming. Dan was waiting for me when I came back, motioning with his head for me to follow him into his office. I stood with my back to the door determined to keep myself calm.

"Just tell me why? Why now? Is leaving me just a way of winning?"

"There is no why, Dan. You always tell me, trust my gut. This is what my gut is telling me."

He shook his head. "I don't believe you. Something must have happened."

"Maybe I'm just bored. I want to move on. I'm really grateful for all that you've taught me, but there's more out there. The world's my playground. I want to test myself, see what I can do."

"I thought we'd go on together – finish this and move on to the next thing together."

"I don't want to always be in your shadow, your follower."

"But this was your idea, always your idea."

"Not the hotel. The hotel is yours."

"Ours. And your grandad's. A joint effort."

"I want something of my own. Just my own."

"There's no such thing, Jo. We don't live in a vacuum. We always need help from other people. Surely you know that."

I turned to go.

"I called Caroline," he said, quickly. "She's arriving tomorrow."

Part of the plan for the hotel, part of the 'live your dreams' plan, was to have an artist in residence – Caroline, of course. She'd work out of the studio, give art lessons to the guests who wanted them, and there would be an apartment for her and Mikey.

I really didn't want to see her just now.

"Why? The apartment won't be ready for another week."

"They can use one of the guest rooms until then. We've put the art lessons in the brochure. Guests have been asking."

I'd just have to face her. But I knew why Dan had called her.

"Nothing she can say will make a difference."

"We'll see. Anyway, I knew she'd be disappointed if you'd gone before she got here."

Did we even have anything in common any more? Something told me she wouldn't like this new me. I knew she wouldn't get who I was now and I didn't want to see any look of disappointment on her face, any trace of disgust. Maybe that's why my going seemed so urgent – I wanted to slip away before she came.

"Tomorrow."

"That's right."

I squared my shoulders. "Okay."

54

The next message was from Malcolm. "Your grandad said you're in trouble."

"I'm not."

"He said you need to see me."

"I don't." As soon as I said it, my body went into turmoil. My stomach turned, my heart started beating fast. "Okay, maybe I do. Do you have any time tomorrow? After two?" I'd get my conversation with Caroline over, then Malcolm could help if I needed calming down.

"Sure. Let's say two thirty."

"Great."

Next it was Grandad, fast to the door when I arrived for dinner that night. "Come over here. There's something I need to say."

"I'm going to see Malcolm, tomorrow."

"This is separate. I want to tell you myself."

I sighed. It seemed a relatively simple decision I had made, like going away to university, and everyone had accepted that. Why all this fuss? "Okay. What is it?"

"Remember in Dan's other hotel we were talking about people helping people. About people not needing to be in trouble to be helped."

"Yes . . ."

"Remember. I want to make sure you understand. Good people help people whatever stage they're at."

I was struggling to get his point. I knew what he was after – to get me to stay. But I didn't understand why and I didn't understand the relevance of what he had said. He read my expression.

"You understand about helping sick people."

"Yes."

"And you understand about helping hungry people."

"Yes."

"And you understand about helping poor people."

"Yes." I strained to keep my impatience in check. Grandad always had a point, and it was always worth waiting for, so I waited, even though I suspected this time it was something I didn't want to hear.

"And you know about helping people who want to do something, but don't have the money, or don't know how."

"Yes, Grandad, I know about that."

I watched his face. He didn't speak for a moment.

"Okay, so go the next step up."

The next step up. From sick to hungry to poor to under-resourced.

"Come on! What's the next step up?"

"Um . . . people who want to do something and do have the money and know-how."

"Yes! That's it!"

"You want me to help . . . who, exactly?"

"Me. And Dan. And everyone."

I closed my eyes again. It felt like a trap. "But what about my dreams, Grandad? What about me?"

"Jo. As far as I can see you don't have any dreams. You are just being a ... a ... spoiled brat."

My eyes opened with a flick, wide and staring. Grandad had never judged me before. He never judged anyone. I turned and walked out the door.

SLOW TIME

55

I spent that night in my old bed, in my dad's house. He made no comment when I came out to breakfast, dressed and ready for work, deep circles under my eyes.

I kissed his forehead on the way out, feeling his eyes on me as I closed the door behind me.

Dan's face showed relief when he saw me at reception, handling the busy checkout time. "I thought you might have gone," he whispered as he passed close by me.

"No. Not yet."

Caro came in at ten. They must have left Wanaka early. I saw concern on her face. She sent Mikey through with the cases to find Dan and inclined her head for me to follow. Might as well get it over with.

We walked down the gravel path to the studio, the silence awkward. I needed her to speak first, but in our relationship it is usually me who drives things.

"Dan says you're leaving."

"Don't I have the right to? I'm not going straight away."

"I thought you loved him."

"You told me not to, remember? You said I couldn't trust him."

"No. I never said that."

"Well, then, you said I was a fool, that he would enjoy me then dump me, move on."

"I didn't say that, either."

"Maybe not in words. But it was clear that was his pattern, and that you feared for me."

"That isn't how it went, though, is it? He loves you. You're going to break his heart."

"Surely not. Surely he's tough, he'll recover. People break up every day. Why is everyone so against this?"

"Because you're in love. You're making a mistake."

I looked into her eyes. She knows me so well, reads me from some silent place inside her and is always right.

"God! Yesterday I felt so powerful, so invincible, so sure. I am still sure I need to move on, do something for myself."

"It's not like you to be so selfish. Look around. Look at what you've created. You wouldn't have any of this if it weren't for Dan."

"He's benefitted, too."

"What does that have to do with it? Why are you throwing it away?"

"It isn't mine!"

"As much as it is anyone's, it is yours. Until you can see that, you can't go. Your life would be empty, you'd be searching forever."

I looked away from her. Her words were echoing around in my head.

"I thought we'd have fun, living here, both of us. I even had dreams of raising our children together, cousins running around on this lawn."

"I'm just finding my strength. I need to stretch myself."

"Just open your eyes, Jo. Everything you need is here. At least wait till you have a plan."

There was still an hour until I was due to see Malcolm. I drove into town and went to borrow Archie. Since I had moved out to the hotel, Dad had taken over his daily walks, but he was delighted to see me, jumping and leaping off the floor. "Come on, Boy. Come see what good you can do me."

It was so automatic, the slowing of my thoughts as I matched my pace to his. This was different than my workouts in the gym. It was more peaceful. What was I looking for, when I announced my half-baked plan? Autonomy. A new project. Freedom. And something else was lurking there, something stronger. I wanted power. The games Dan and I had been playing had reached this ultimate end. It was like a game of chess. Not making this move would be like ignoring the opportunity of checkmate, to decide to leave the game running forever, or until my opponent saw his opportunity and took it himself. I never doubted he would. I hadn't expected the opportunity to be mine.

Now I thought about it, it seemed an odd metaphor for a relationship. "Life's a game, Jo. Just a game." It had hurt so much to hear him say it.

SLOW TIME

56

I tied up Archie at Malcolm's door and gave him some biscuits to keep him happy. I hoped I wouldn't be long inside.

"There you are. I'm glad to see you."

I stepped into the house, shivering in the darkness that cloaked in as he closed the door to the unlit hall. There didn't seem to be any heating on.

"Now, what is it?"

"It's not fair!" I burst out. "I don't understand what's happening. I did everything, for everyone, and now everyone wants to stop me doing something for me."

Malcolm just watched me, infuriating calm in his eyes.

"Why shouldn't I go if I want to? Why shouldn't I follow my dreams?"

"And what are they?"

I was silent. I looked into the unlit grate of his fireplace and shuddered with cold.

"What are they? Jo?"

"They're so big I can't describe them! They're so huge no-one would understand. They're so unique they cannot be put into words." Somewhere in my mind a memory echoed, a similar scene from a decade and a half ago.

It seemed I had been arguing with adults all my life for my individuality, for my brilliance, and none of them would listen or understand.

"Then tell me about the dreams you've had that have come true. You've saved the town, and everyone in it. Tell me about that."

"That's history. That's done. Old news."

"It's not done until you learn from it. So tell me what you've learned."

I shifted my feet mutinously, but actually his question interested me. What had I learned? "Lots of things. Lots. About building and web-sites and hotels and the Internet and food and entertainment and what makes life worthwhile."

"And what does make life worthwhile?"

"People," I said, surprising myself. "People like you."

"So what happened?"

"I wanted power. I wanted to win."

"True power comes from . . ."

"Helping people," I finished for him. "And being true to myself." I paused for a moment, thinking. "But I thought I was. It's okay to be ambitious. Isn't it?"

"Yes."

"But?"

"You tell me."

"But I have to balance all of life. And I have to be able to live with myself."

57

I went back home embarrassed. I would have to face Dan sooner or later, but I took the coward's way out, sneaking up to our room and hoping he didn't find me for hours. It backfired. He was there, sitting in a chair staring out the window.

He turned, startled. "You're back. I thought you might not be coming back." Then he laughed. "I think I've said that before, haven't I?"

"Yup."

"You don't look like you're going. Are you staying?"

"I don't know. I don't know anything."

"But you aren't leaving me?"

"I need to work out what I'm doing."

"Well, can you do that here? Can I help you?"

"Maybe."

"What are you thinking? Do you have any ideas?"

"Maybe a new project. Maybe write up what's happened here. Yes, maybe that. Really get to understand it."

"It's a miracle what you've done here."

"Do you really think so?"

"I know it is."

"It's funny. It seemed so huge, so impossible, and then once it was done it felt like nothing at all."

"It's not nothing."

"No. It's really something. I know."

I don't know when they did it, or how they did it without me suspecting.

The next day, the old spark of mischief was back in Dan's eyes, the old laughing confidence. He lured me up to our suite, and, wow, kept me in bed all afternoon. My heart stops even at the memory. Then later, as the sun went down behind the mountains, he tousled my hair, told me to get dressed, he wanted to go downstairs to the restaurant to celebrate.

"Didn't we just spend the last four hours celebrating. God! What was that?"

"Humour me. Look sexy. Drive the patrons wild. Who knows, it might be just the thing that has them coming back year after year. I know it would me."

I frowned at him, puzzled. This was a new mood.

I let him pick out a slim black dress, split to the hip, plunging back and neckline. I imagined imagining myself wearing this, only a year ago. It would have been unthinkable. "Okay." I put it on, brushed my teeth, looked at myself in the mirror. My cheeks were flushed. "Everyone will know," I protested.

He grinned wide. "I know."

He took my hand and led me downstairs, stopping at the restaurant door to kiss me again. He pulled back, looking deep into my eyes. "You've been asking what is missing in your life. I think I know what it is."

"What?"

"Celebration. Acknowledging your achievements."

"But I did, I have. I told you, I know it's something."

"But you haven't really celebrated." He turned and pushed the door open. "Not till now."

There was a huge shout, a cheer, and paper streamers came flying at me. I stood completely still, staring at everyone I cared about in the world. Grandad came running. "Look, Jo, they've come to say thank you! It was Caroline's idea!"

I looked down at my black, sexy dress, feeling so out of place. Tears were streaming, I felt arm after arm around me, hugging, lips on my cheeks. When I looked up, I saw Caroline, crying too. Behind her was a banner. "Thank you for saving Folkstown, Jo. We love you!"

Louise pulled me out of the way of the others. "I'm so sorry, Jo. For being so stubborn, so ungrateful. I knew how much it took, for you to do what you did. I was just too wrapped up in myself to admit it."

Dad came up behind her. "Me, too. You need to know what a miracle you've been, for me, for all of us."

I frowned, trying to hold back more tears. Nothing like this had ever happened in my life before. Everything, every achievement, had meant nothing more than the signal to move on. As I looked around the room, at all the smiling, beloved faces, it began to sink in. I had made a difference. I had helped. And now it was time to celebrate, and accept their thanks.

"Here." It was Dan. "Time for you to make a speech."

"Oh, no!"

He gestured to Jason, and between the two of them they lifted me onto a table. Louise tapped her glass and everyone went quiet.

"What is there to say? What should I say?" No-one was helping me. I looked around from one to another. They waited, expectantly, patiently. I'd have to think of something to say. "As a whole town, you raised me. You're the most inspiring people I know. I came home to find the town struggling – what could I do but help it back on its feet? You've all been patient, indulgent, like you have been all my life. Thank you for telling me I've made a difference, and thank you for helping me to make that difference. It has been a privilege, working alongside you all." It was really sinking in, the oddest feeling, euphoric, but grounding as well.

Someone shouted from the back of the crowd – maybe it was Peter, or James. "So now that you've got us sorted, what are you going to do?"

I looked around. The urge to run was gone, leaving peace behind it. I held my hand out for Dan, pulled him up on the table next to me. "I'm not sure. Mind if I stick around here for a while until I figure it out?"

Caroline clapped. Dan leaned in and kissed me, and the room erupted in another deafening cheer.

~ ~ ~ ~ ~ ~ ~ ~ ~ ~ ~ ~ ~ ~ ~

If you have enjoyed

Slow Time

Please email jennifer@jennifermanson.co.nz
to join my mailing list and receive information
about further publications, or see
www.jennifermanson.co.nz.

I welcome your feedback.

Please post your review on Facebook.
Search for "Jennifer Manson Author"

With my very great thanks,

Jennifer.

www.ingramcontent.com/pod-product-compliance
Lightning Source LLC
Chambersburg PA
CBHW070635260626
47161CB00007B/2714